Demons Unfolding

Bella Skaja

PUBLISHED BY

SIGMA'S
BOOKSHELF

MINNETONKA, MN 55305
WWW.SIGMASBOOKSHELF.COM

I dedicate this book to Hannah, Lidya, and Miss Tara Lorence, my theater teacher and idol.

Phrases Used in This Book

Eagle Spirit = the tribe's supreme being
Aur = Gold
Bwyta = Consume

Chapter 1

A rustle in a nearby bush caught my eye. I carefully drew back my bow string and waited. In hunting, the one thing you must have is patience. The bush rustled again. This time, a deer emerged from the brush. *WHOOSH!* My arrow flew through the air, piercing the animal straight through the neck. It died in mid air and fell like a rock into the river. I slung my bow over my shoulder and began to heave the deer to my tribal village, Ashinders.

I passed the garden where all our crops grow, and my little sister, Moonlight, waved at me. She, along with some other women, was helping my mother harvest the wheat. "Welcome back!" she exclaimed. I just rolled my eyes at her and continued to heave my game to the market.

I pulled the deer onto the game dealer's booth. After waiting a half hour in the hot afternoon sun for a deer to finally come along, I expected big money.

The game dealer studied the deer, then finally looked at me and answered, "Ten silver bits." My mouth dropped open in disbelief. Anger welled up in my throat. "Ten bits?"

"Take it or leave it," he said, holding out ten silver coins to me. Frustrated, I snatched the coins out of his palm and walked away from the booth. As I headed home, someone said, "I would have paid thirty bits for the venison that you just provided."

I whipped my head around. "Oh! Good evening, Trout Skin," I said to the woman standing in front of me. She had gray hair pulled back into a loose bun. When she smiled, she had dimples that aligned with her slightly crooked nose.

"Don't take offense to this, but thirty bits is three quarters of your money."

Trout Skin laughed. "That venison would have fed my family for a week! I would have paid forty-five bits for that much!"

I smiled and nodded. "I will keep that in mind for my next catch. Have a good rest of your day, Trout Skin."

I was almost home when I came upon the river. I walked to it and looked around, hoping no one was there. When I didn't see anyone I thought to myself, *I guess a quick bathing wouldn't hurt.* I began to strip off my clothes when I heard a voice. "Hazelnut?"

I screamed and rushed to put my dress back on. I turned around and threw my fist into the person's stomach. He crumpled to the ground groaning. Once he recovered, I saw his face. I gasped. "Blue Fox?" The boy looked into my face.

His cow brown eyes complimented his jet-black hair. He was a muscular, handsome, young boy. His skin was the color of thick, fresh maple syrup. I will always remember the mole right below his left temple.

"By Eagle Spirit's name, are you alright?" After I was fully clothed, I rushed over to where Blue Fox had keeled over. "What can I do to—" I stood up and looked at him angrily. "Why did you come over here anyway?"

Blue Fox groaned for a bit before also standing up. He was about an inch or so taller than me. "It is your turn to bathe in the well today if you would like to," he said rather hastily.

I pondered this offer. It would be rather nice to take a hot bath, compared to the ice-cold water of the river, but Blue Fox probably needed it more.

"You can have it," I said.

Blue Fox looked confused. "Have what?"

"My bath. I don't need it, really. I just took one yesterday and—"

"I get it," Blue Fox spat.

I got the feeling that he was very upset with me for punching him in the gut. I guess I would be upset with him if he were to punch me.

"Well, have a good rest of your day, Blue Fox."

As I walked back to the path home, I heard Blue Fox say, "Yeah, you as well."

When I got home, I took the scene in. Our small oak shack emitted the aroma of buffalo stew, carrying the feeling of comfort and joy. The house was divided into three parts: the living room and kitchen, my parent's room, and Moonlight's and my room.

My mother stepped out of the shack and smiled. "You arrived just in time for dinner." I stepped inside the shack and something small barreled into me.

"Hazel! Hazel! I found a green onion in the wheat patch today!" said Moonlight. She was ten years old, curious, clever, and wanted nothing more than to impress me.

"Good for you!" I said in a fake, cheery tone.

"Mom put it in the stew!" Moonlight exclaimed. She started to bounce up and down.

Mother had started pouring stew into clay bowls. "Come, come. Let's eat."

Me and Moony sat down at our small wooden table. Moonlight looked up at Mother. "Mother, are buffalo important?"

Mother giggled, "Oh, yes! They provide us with food, tools, clothing, and much more. They are the key to our survival."

Moony frowned at her soup bowl. "So without buffalo, we would all be dead?"

"I wouldn't say that. I think it would be fairly difficult to survive without them, but enough! Eat your soup!"

After dinner, mother put Moonlight to bed. I was heading outside to wash my face when mother stopped me. "We need to talk."

I sat down on our cotton chair. Mother sat across from me on a buffalo fur chair.

I sighed, "Mother, if you are going to pester me about hunting again—"

"Desert Flower is missing," mother said blankly.

For a second, I thought I had misheard her. Desert Flower was my best friend. People called us twins. She couldn't possibly be missing, could she?

"When did s-she disappear?"

"Yesterday afternoon."

"And you didn't bother telling me last night?" I demanded.

"Hazel, I didn't find out until this morning, and since you were out hunting," she sighed. I wanted to say something to her, an apology or something, but no words came out of my mouth.

Mother stood up. "Time for bed, then."

I slowly got to my feet. "Alright."

I pulled on my satin nightgown that Desert Flower's mother had bought me on my 16th moonday. I was still in great shock.

Desert Flower was missing.

I got into bed. As I pulled up the covers, something ran through my head. It wasn't about Desert Flower. Mother had talked with me yesterday morning. She had said that as an eighteen-year-old woman, it was time to start thinking about my spouse.

It was the tradition of our tribe for women to get married at eighteen. I had complained that it wasn't fair, that I should be able to choose when to marry. But mother had reasoned that I should feel fortunate that I had the freedom to choose my spouse. She had said that it would be nice to have Blue Fox as a son-in-law, and I had cheerily smirked at her.

As I closed my eyes, a figure came into my mind. A girl. Her short caramel hair was being blown into her dark brown eyes. She had a lovely shaped olive face. The girl was very, very beautiful, but something in her eyes made her look sad. And I knew that face.

Desert Flower.

Suddenly, she screamed. A large, red cloud of mist formed around her and when it had cleared, Desert Flower was gone.

Chapter 2

*K*nock, knock. My eyes flew open.
Knock, knock.
"One moment please!" Mother shouted from her room.

Moony was still sleeping. Her chest rose and fell with grace, a small smile on her face. The only thing that disturbed the serenity of Moony's sleep was the sound coming out of her mouth. It sounded like a grizzly bear's roar. Mother said the city folk called it 'snoring'.

I got out of bed and trudged to the kitchen just as mother said to the person at the door, "Thank you, Red Robin. I will send her down after the morning meal." She handed the messenger five bronze coins.

"Well you have a good rest of your day, Nightingale," he said, and with a greedy grin he put the coins into his satchel and walked toward the market.

Mother closed the door. "After the morning meal, go down to the infirmary. Father will meet you there. No questions asked."

I was astonished at how grim her face and voice were. "Alright," I replied.

The morning meal wasn't anything special; quail eggs and fresh, warm bread. I love the smell of bread fresh out of the oven.

I was just about to leave when Moony came out of our

room, still in her nightgown. "Where are you going, Hazel?" she asked sleepily.

Mother handed her a plate of eggs and toast. "Just going exploring. You should eat. Remember you are going to the river today with Lily."

Moonlight took the plate from Mother's hands, sat down at the table, and began eating.

I grabbed my bow and quiver from my chest in my room and waved goodbye to Mother and Moonlight. I stepped out of the door and walked down the cobblestone road leading through the market and to the infirmary.

The infirmary was a large wooden building with four glass windows on each of its four sides. The interior was basically two rows of beds going down each side. Each bed had cotton blankets on it and an individual nightstand. There were curtains separating the beds from one another.

I stepped into the infirmary and the first thing that I saw was my father; a middle aged man with black eyes and straight, shoulder length black hair. The only thing unfamiliar about father was that he had heavy bandages around his torso and leg.

I rushed over to his bed. "Father! What happened?" I exclaimed. He set his beetle black eyes on me.

"Just a hunting accident," he said plainly. "A grizzly caught us off guard. No man died, but three were seriously hurt, including me." He gestured to two men in hospital beds.

"Father, you must be more careful. Remember Mother's rule?"

"'Always expect the unexpected.' Hazelnut, I have been hunting since I was ten years old; my mother repeated that rule everyday. I will remember it until my death day." Father smiled. I smiled back.

I lifted my head. A peculiar smell filled my nose. I knew that smell. *Smoke.*

Without a word of goodbye or warning to father, I ran to the infirmary's entrance. I couldn't see Ashinders, but I knew by heart how to get there through the trees and thicket.

As I ran toward the village, more and more smoke filled my nostrils. I was almost to the village when I saw Blue Fox's sister, Ocean Lotus, running toward me. Her black hair was being blown into her face as she ran. "Hazelnut! Hazelnut! The demons, they have come!"

Chapter 3

The demons. I had thought they were a myth. My mother used to tell me stories about them.

They live in an underground chamber, the demons. They are similar to me and you. The demons have human bodies, but large, leathery, batlike wings. Their skin is blood red and thick, like buffalo hide, and from their heads, small pointy horns, similar to bull horns, sprout. They breathe the heat of one thousand suns. They were all male, except for the mother demon, who owned the throne. After she had given birth to twenty little demons of her own, her eldest son, Redskin, killed her. He then took the throne and still rules today.

I used to enjoy these stories when I was small. As I ran down the cobblestone road, I realized just how real demons were. There were about five demons total, dive-bombing the village. People were screaming, children were crying, and the demons were laughing while setting shacks on fire. I recognized the messenger, Red Robin, running toward me. "HELP ME! HELP ME!" Red Robin was seized under the arms by a demon. The demon flew towards the Black Mountains, a place where no one comes back from.

I took out my bow and notched an arrow. I aimed at a demon that was about to attack Trout Skin. The arrow struck him in the right shoulder blade. That got his attention. He turned his ugly face toward me. I expected him to run and seize me and take me to the Black Mountains, like Red Robin, but he slowly lumbered toward me.

He was about ten feet away when a small rock hit him in the head. Until then, I had been staring with fear at the demon, but now, both me and the demon turned our attention to the person who threw the rock.

My heart seemed to have stopped beating. The little girl who had thrown the rock held another in her hand. Tears began to well in my eyes. The girl was Moonlight.

"MOONLIGHT!" I screamed. "YOU FOOL! RUN!"

But the demon was now hurtling towards her. She kept throwing rocks at him, but they harmlessly bounced off of his hide.

"If I bring you to Chief Redskin, I will be greatly rewarded." His voice was deep, like a bear's roar.

Tears of fear were now in Moony's eyes as well.

I fired another arrow at the demon; he was now only a few feet away from my little sister. One after another, I shot. My last arrow flew into his calf, which made him stumble. He whipped his head around. "I have had mercy on you. The Chief would gladly have you as well, but the littler ones are harder to get," he snarled.

He picked me up with his right hand, Moonlight in his left, and threw me into a nearby oak. My chest was the first thing to make contact with the tree, then my whole upper torso. I slid down the tree onto my leg. So many things happened at once.

A ferocious pain shot through my right leg, my vision went blurry. I could hear Moonlight screaming, I could make out her body and the demon's. He held her with one hand, and with the other swatted off anyone daring to try and rescue my sister.

I tried very hard to stand and help, but just moving my

right leg made me feel nauseous. The demon flew into the air and, as he flew off to the mountains, set fire to a shack.

The tears were streaming down my face with the fierceness of a rushing waterfall. I poured every last droplet of my strength into my leg. I *needed* to go after her; to go after Moonlight, but I could not stand; so I began to drag myself toward the mountains.

Someone rushed over to me. For a moment, I thought that they were going to help me get to Moonlight, but they grabbed my forearm and pulled me into their lap.

"There is no more we can do, Hazel. She is gone," said my mother's voice.

Her tears splashed onto my forehead, then ran down the bridge of my nose and into my eyes. They mixed with my own tears and trickled down my face.

"I refuse to believe that all hope is lost." I tried to pull my arm out of my mother's grasp, but she was strong and held fast.

"I want to believe that too, Hazel, but she is gone."

Fear and sorrow were suddenly replaced with anger. I pulled myself up and turned to face her. "How can you say that? She is *your* daughter. You can't give up that easily, Mother," I shouted. Mother let go of my arm.

I again attempted to stand, forgetting that my leg was broken. As soon as I moved my right leg, my vision swam. I felt a sudden desire to hurl and I collapsed onto the grass. I fought with all of my might to stay conscious; but I lost.

The last thing I remember seeing was two figures running to my side. Then everything went dark.

"SHE IS GOING TO BE alright, then?"

"Yes, Nightingale."

"I just can't lose her, doctor."

"I understand that, but—"

"First Moonlight, and then her father," sobbed a woman.

"I understand that you and Hazelnut are grieving greatly, but Eagle Spirit had these things happen for a reason," said a deep-voiced male.

"I understand that, doctor. Thank you for coming and I give my blessing to your daughter."

"And mine to yours."

The door closed.

My eyes fluttered open. My right leg was numb and heavy; it was thickly wrapped in bandages. When I tried to move it, it felt as heavy as a buffalo's hide.

I was in my bed, in me and Moonlight's room.

Moonlight.

Suddenly, everything came back to me: father in the infirmary, the demons' attack, Moonlight's abduction.

I climbed out of bed and limped to the kitchen. Mother was staring out the window when I walked in. She didn't even look at me when she said, "There is tea and bread on the table. I would like you to eat."

"Alright." I walked over to the table, sat down, and took a bite of the warm bread. It tasted like heaven. I ate half of the loaf before mother took the bread away from me. Then I drank the tea. I had not had tea many times, because I was not very fond of it; but the warm drink felt wonderful as it ran down my throat.

I suddenly remembered Mother and the doctor's conversation. "Is father healing up well?" I asked.

Mother looked up from her tea that she was pouring, "Y-your father, h-he is—not well."

"When will he get better?"

"I don't—" she turned to look at me. Tears suddenly started pouring from her eyes. "Hazel, I don't know how to tell you—your father, he is—he is—"

"Dead," I finished for her. "Right?" I knew the answer before the words left my mouth. "How?"

"Oh, Hazel! The wound from the bear got infected and spread." Mother ran to my side, pulled me into a tight embrace, and began weeping into my shoulder. In a matter of seconds, my shoulder was drenched with her tears; my face wet with my own.

"We have Eagle Spirit's blessing, right?"

"I hope we do, Hazel, I—" Someone knocked on the door.

Mother got up and walked to the entryway. She grabbed the handle and slowly opened the door.

Ocean Lotus stood in the doorway with a small buffalo hide sack slung over her shoulder. "Mrs. Nightingale, my mother sent me over to ask if I could stay with you." Ocean Lotus didn't make eye contact. "Just until my shack is rebuilt," she added.

Mother wiped the tears out of her eyes and gestured to the living room. "Welcome to our home, Ocean Lotus."

Ocean Lotus stepped over the threshold and Mother closed the door.

Chapter 4

Ocean Lotus shared a room with me. She insisted on sleeping on the floor, but I told her that she was welcome to sleep on Moonlight's bed. She declined the offer.

I visited the infirmary three times a week for three weeks. My leg healed up pretty quickly, considering that the first doctor said it would never heal, but he had only been working as a doctor for three weeks.

We buried my father two days after his death, next to a bed of fiery red snapdragons. Mother and I then planted a small beech tree on top of his grave. Mother said that the tree roots will wrap around his body and carry him to the afterlife, where he will come back as another life form.

As we walked down the cobblestone road, watching the shacks be rebuilt and letting the rain fall onto our faces, I said, "A stag," not realizing that I was thinking out loud.

Mother turned to face me, "A stag?"

"Father once told me that when he dies, he will come back to life as a stag."

Mother sighed. "He never told me that."

"You would not have been entertained by his thoughts, Mother." I grinned and continued to walk to our shack.

As my mother and I approached our shack, there was a wonderful scent coming from between the oak planks. Mother stopped dead in her tracks; I ran straight to the shack door and threw it open.

Ocean Lotus was wearing a crocheted apron and mixing green onions into a pot of a bubbling something. She looked up and smiled.

"I thought I would take some stress off of your mother's shoulders and make dinner."

At that moment, mother walked into the shack and stared at Ocean Lotus, "Er—thank you, O-Ocean Lotus."

"Anytime, Nightingale," she said, looking up from the pot. "Is it alright if I call you that?"

Mother nodded then said, "I hope you know, Ocean Lotus, that I truly appreciate your cooking dinner. It will give me the chance to sleep." Without even saying good-night, mother walked into her room and closed the door.

"I will save some soup for tomorrow," Ocean Lotus said softly, "in case she wants a quick meal." She dished out two bowls of soup and handed one to me. We sat down at the table.

"How was the burial?" Ocean Lotus asked into her bowl.

"I thought it would be the same as your grandmother's burial but at father's, I actually cried," I replied.

We finished the rest of our soup in silence. Ocean Lotus washed the bowls in the river while I prepared for bed.

I was just getting into bed when Ocean Lotus walked into the room and began to change into her nightdress.

She washed her hair and laid down on her makeshift bed.

"I insist that you sleep in," I paused, "in Moonlight's bed."

"No," Ocean Lotus said.

I was getting very frustrated with her for being so stubborn. "For the love of Eagle Spirit, just do it! It is a bed! Moonlight is not going to care! When she returns—"

"*If* she returns," Ocean Lotus interrupted.

"You are just as hopeless as mother is!" I screamed. I no longer cared if I woke Mother. I didn't care if I woke the whole village. I wanted people to have hope.

"If I sleep in Moonlight's bed, will you sleep in mine?"
I barked.

"Yes."

"Okay!" I threw off the covers and pulled a spare blanket
out of my chest. I walked to the living room and shut the
door to my room. I laid down on the buffalo fur couch and
fell into an unpleasant sleep.

I did not dream. I enjoyed that after three weeks of
nightmares.

I woke the next morning and smelled smoke. The demons.
I hurried to get out of bed, remembered I had slept on the
couch, and fell off of the couch. Someone laughed. I looked
up. Ocean Lotus was looking down at me. The scent of
smoke was coming from the stove. Ocean Lotus had already
prepared the morning meal.

I remembered the spat we had last night. (Or more like
me yelling at her for not sleeping in a decent bed). I know
it was unfair of me but her humility was frustrating at times.

I slowly stood up, as if she would knock me to the ground
again any moment. "Look," I began. The big grin slowly
slid off of her face. "I am sorry for yelling at you last night.
With everything going on in my family—"

"It is quite alright," Ocean Lotus replied kindly. "Blue Fox
tries not to yell at me, but I can be annoying at times, so—"

"I'm going hunting after I eat. Want to come?" I asked.

"Oh no. I do not support the killing of innocent animals,"
she said as she set a bowl of mush on the table. "Eat."

I sat down at the table and stared at the mush. "What
is this?" I asked.

"It's oats and warm milk. I call it oatmeal."

After the meal, I walked down the cobblestone road to
the forest. The sun was just rising over the Black Mountains
and the air was not too cold, yet not too warm.

I was just admiring some new weaponry about halfway

into the market when someone walked straight into me and knocked my arrows out my quiver. "Oh!" I exclaimed. "Blue Fox!"

"I am so sorry, Hazel, I did not see you there. Well, more like I was not paying attention," Blue Fox apologized.

He helped me pick up my arrows. I had twelve arrows in all. Five of them had broken when they fell out of my quiver.

"Oh, Hazel! Let me buy you new arrows at the weaponry," Blue Fox said. I did not protest.

Blue Fox bought me fifteen arrows for fifteen silver bits.

"Would you want to go hunting with me?" I asked. "It would just be until the sun peaks."

Blue Fox grinned. "I have not hunted for a week at least." When I stared at him blankly he added, "I would love to."

We walked to the forest and on the way, Blue Fox grabbed his bow, full quiver, and a silver dagger. A dagger that gave off a faint red glow, like the red mist in my dream.

Chapter 5

We walked for fifteen minutes and didn't see a single bird, rabbit, butterfly, insect, basically any living, breathing thing.

I started to get curious. "Where is every—" A giant winged creature swiftly flew overhead.

"What kind of bird was that?" I asked Blue Fox; not that he was the cleverest fox or anything. He did not answer. He just stared into the sky where the creature had flown above.

"Nevermind," I snapped. I was getting annoyed with Blue Fox for being so mysterious.

"Stay here," I commanded.

Blue Fox didn't acknowledge that I spoke to him. I sighed.

I began to climb a nearby oak. *Skillfully* climb it, if I do say so myself. When I reached the treetop, I poked my head through the canopy. The view I found was spectacular. I could see the tops of market booths in Ashinders, and the rivers and mountains in the distance. But something was strange.

I now noticed that the giant winged creature was a demon, and that there were about ten of them standing in a circle one-hundred feet away from us. In hindsight, I should have probably ran instead of watching the gathering. The demons seemed to be waiting for someone.

Another demon, bigger than the rest, swooped in and landed with grace just outside of the demons' circle. I noticed a large, black beaded necklace around his neck.

As soon as he landed, all of the other demons did a sort of salute. "Chief Redskin," they said in unison. They made room for the chief in the circle. When everyone stopped shifting about and was comfortable, the chief spoke.

"As you all know, we have not yet succeeded in transferring the magic into a living life form." His voice was very deep and surprisingly terrifying. "My son, however, proved himself worthy of being one of us. He found a magical being." All of the demons cheered. "When he told me this, nearly ten years ago, I gave him the power to change his appearance at his will. Since then he has been bringing information to me about the being. She is one of the natives; lives in a village called Ashinders, which is right over there." Redskin pointed the direction to the village. "I will not speak her name."

"Why, sir?" a demon interrupted.

Redskin turned his head toward the demon. "Why? Because I simply don't want to and if you interrupt or question me again, you will become as dead as the other attempted vessels, understand?"

"Y-yes, Ch-Chief Redskin," the demon whimpered.

"Good. Now, as I was saying, my son is still with her at this very moment, and we are going to get her this time, because he will stop her from running; and if I am interrupted again." He paused. "Alright, here is the plan: once I am finished talking, we will split up and find the girl. Use your nose to smell out my son; do not kill unless absolutely necessary. Then, once you get the girl, whoever that might be, you signal the others. Fly her back to the mountains. Leave the girl to me; do not do anything to her unless I tell you to, or I will kill you and throw your carcass to the birds."

The other demons all nodded fearfully.

"Please, Chief, tell us her name." Everyone turned to the

demon who had spoken. I noticed he was the smallest one at the gathering.

"Why?" Redskin demanded. I was shocked that he did not kill the demon on the spot.

"Maybe her name might give us some clues as to her appearance, unless you know that as well."

"I do not know what she looks like, and you do have a point. Her name—" all of the demons were anxious to hear it. I was too. "is—"

Crack.

I looked down. The branch I was standing on was beginning to break. "B-Blue Fox!" I whispered.

Blue Fox had been looking at the demons from the ground. He now looked up at me. "Move very slowly towards the bough."

I very slowly shuffled toward the bough as he told me to do. I was inches away, but not close enough to reach the bough, when the whole branch broke off. I panicked and jumped towards the bough. I missed but my right hand managed to grab hold of another small branch. My knee cap slammed into the trunk of the tree. I wanted to scream in agony as loud as I could, but I couldn't, not with how close the demons were.

Blue Fox had disappeared. I held on to the branch for as long as I could. I could no longer see where Blue Fox was and my grip on the branch was dwindling. I was going to die.

When I tried to bring my left hand up to the branch, my right hand slipped. That was it, I was going to fall fifteen feet, break my leg again, scream, get caught by the demons, and die.

I was beginning to imagine my death when someone's hand grabbed mine and heaved me up into the bough.

When I was safely in the bough, Blue Fox hugged me. It felt good to be hugged, after everything that was going on.

"We need to run, now. Get on my back," he said.

Blue Fox picked me up and swung me onto his back; my hands loosely around his neck and my left leg tightly around his waist. He climbed down the tree with such ease, my tree climbing skills looked like a toddler's in comparison.

As soon as we reached the ground, I climbed off of Blue Fox's back and we ran like the North Wind to Ashinders. The only problem was that we ran into a demon on the way there.

We were not looking where we were running and we collided with it. He was not a small demon either. He was at least one-and-a-half times my size. Once he saw I was with Blue Fox, he lunged for me. Blue Fox unsheathed his dagger, stepped in front of me, and made a deep cut across the demon's face.

The demon roared in pain. "I thought you would know better than to injure your own."

Another roar of pain. Blue Fox had thrown his dagger into the demon's right leg.

"Come on!" Blue Fox grabbed my hand and we ran deeper into the forest.

For a moment, I thought we had escaped the demons, but then one soared overhead. I lost focus to where I was running and my foot hooked on an exposed tree root. I fell to the ground and hit my head on a large rock. Then everything went blurry. Blue Fox had not realized I had fallen and kept running until a demon landed in front of him. He tried to go right, a demon blocked him; left, the same. "Hazel, we are trapped. Hazel?" He finally realized that I was laying on the forest floor. I knew for a fact that the fall had broken my leg again. We were surrounded by demons and I was losing consciousness.

Blue Fox seemed to be trying to reason with the demons, but one demon shoved him aside and walked to where I lay. As the demon approached where I lay, I did my best to escape but my broken leg would not allow so much as a twitch without unbearable pain ensuing. He unhooked my leg from the tree root. I soon felt my body being lifted into the air before the world around me went pitch-black.

Chapter 6

I woke laying on a cold stone floor. My eyes took a while to adjust to the darkness.

I was in a cell. All that was in the room was a wooden slab that was intended to be a bed chained horizontally to the stone wall. Stone bars separated me from the long desolate hallway. The walkway was dimly lit and I couldn't see the right end of it, but could make out a stone staircase on the left side.

My hair had fallen out of its braid and now lay down by my waist.

"Blue Fox?" I called quietly. No response. "Blue Fox?" I called more loudly. My voice quivered this time.

I crawled to the corner opposite of the 'bed', curled up into a ball and began silently weeping. I was in a strange place, alone, with no food and no source of warmth.

Something interesting popped into my head. I never used to pass out, but ever since the demons began attacking, I was passing out more and more. I think it might have been from fear, or maybe from—

A bat flew out of a crevice in the wall and over my head, almost hitting me. I gasped and covered my head with my hands.

I believe I cried myself to sleep that night; well, I couldn't actually tell whether the moon was awake, or the sun was. The dungeon did not have any windows; the occasional draft came in from the staircase at the end of the hallway.

I stayed in that cell for days it seemed. I slept at the end of each day (or whenever I felt like it), and everytime I woke up, a plate of food was waiting for me just within the stone bars. The meals mostly consisted of a chunk of burnt meat, a puddle of pale mush (that definitely was NOT oatmeal), and a bushy green that tasted like a deer's feces. The only thing that was enjoyable was the drink they gave me; it tasted sweet like honey. I never saw the deliverer, nor did I see Blue Fox. I began to wonder if he was gone, like Desert Flower. Like Moonlight. It was days until I saw another living person.

I was rebraiding my hair when I heard murmuring.

"We were told to bring the girl straight to Redskin's chamber!" said a deep voice.

"No, you fool! We bring her to the possession chamber!" said a high-pitched voice.

"Redskin!"

"Possession!"

"REDSKIN!"

"POSSESSION!"

The two argued until they reached my cell. The deep voiced man was a demon; a tall, muscular demon with big brown horns sprouting above his ears. The high voiced demon looked much like the other one, except that he was very thin and his skin was much darker than the first demon.

"We will bring her to Redskin's chamber," the first demon growled menacingly.

"Fine! Let's do that, Blueblood," said the second demon reluctantly.

They both turned to look at me. "You heard that?" the second demon asked me. The first demon, Blueblood, elbowed him. "Do not speak to the prisoner, Blackblood! Let's bring her to Redskin before we end up like Redvein."

Blueblood waved his hand and the stone bars of my cell

sunk into the ground. Both demons stepped into my cell and pulled me to my feet. It was no use struggling; they were both very strong and I wanted to get out of the cell anyway.

As we walked out of my cell, the stone bars replaced themselves above the ground. The demons led me down the hallway, up the stone staircase, and down another hallway. This hallway was lit more than the dungeon hallway and a long red carpet covered the floor.

I was too busy observing the hallway to notice that we had stopped in front of a large spruce door. Blueblood knocked with his fist. We waited. Both of my escorts seemed very antsy and nervous to be in this position. Another demon opened the door barely an inch, but when he saw me, flung it open wide. "Come in," he grunted.

Blueblood and Blackblood stepped into the room and closed the door. It was a large stone chamber; empty except for two couches facing each other and a coffee table in between them. About seven demons stood in the shadows of the chamber's walls, nothing visible except a faint outline of their bodies and their glowing eyes, which made the scene more terrifying than it already was.

But the person who gave me hope stood before my eyes: Blue Fox. The demons threw me at Blue Fox, hoping to knock him to the floor, but Blue Fox caught me in his muscular arms and pulled me into a tight embrace. I hugged him back; I had thought he was dead. I silently began to weep tears of joy. "I thought you were dead," I whispered.

"But I *knew* that you were alive. I had hope," he whispered back.

"Blue Fox, What is going to happen?" I looked up into his cow brown eyes.

"I do not know. Are you afraid?"

"Yes, Blue Fox. I am afraid. These demons took Desert Flower and Moonlight. We are going to die, just—"

Boom! The spruce door slammed shut once again. Me and Blue Fox looked at the doorway.

I recognized the tall figure of Redskin. Here, I guess it was Chief Redskin. A ray of sunlight caught on the black beaded necklace he was wearing and shone into my eyes.

Now that I was closer to him, I got a better look at his features. He was taller and more muscular than the other demons. He had very short jet black hair and red eyes that were almost brown. His face reminded me of Blue Fox's.

"Leave us." When he spoke, waves of terror rippled off of his skin. The other demons obeyed and left the room without a second glance.

"Child, do you know why I have brought you here?" he asked me in his baritone like voice.

I looked into his eyes, but quickly looked away again. "No, I—"

"She is not a child," Blue Fox interrupted.

Redskin had been staring at me, but now rested his red eyes on Blue Fox. "And who are you to correct me?"

"I am Blue Fox of Ashinders, son of Red Wolf and Blue River, brother of Ocean Lotus, and you will not touch Hazel, or you will answer to me." Blue Fox spoke with such ferocity that the room's temperature seemed to rapidly increase.

"Well, *Blue Fox*, you seem to have grown so fond of this *child* over the years that you—"

"SHUT UP!" Blue Fox screamed. "SHUT UP, YOU FOOL OF A DEMON!"

Redskin's eyes narrowed and his expression grew angry. "Blackblood!" The demon came into the room.

"Yes sir?"

"Take the girl back to her cell. Leave the boy with me." He said this without taking his eyes off of Blue Fox.

"Please," I pleaded, "don't hurt him." I tried to hold back

the tears that were welling in my eyes. Blackblood had now pulled me to my feet and was slowly walking me to the door.

"Haven't you ever loved someone?" I cried out. Blackblood suddenly stopped. I did too.

Redskin now lifted his eyes from Blue Fox's and slowly moved to mine. "Blackblood, did I not tell you to bring her to her cell?"

Fury rose inside me. Blackblood had started to pull me to the door again, but he did it very slowly. "I asked you a question and if you have any dignity, you will answer me!" I demanded.

Redskin turned away from me. Silence. Blackblood now walked faster towards the door. As we stepped over the threshold and into the hallway, I thought I heard Redskin mutter, "Yes."

Chapter 7

Once again I was back in my cell: sleeping on a wooden slab, three meals of meat, mush, and slush a day. I was bored out of my mind and dreamed only of sorrow.

Most of the time I sat braiding and unbraiding my hair or drawing things in the dust on the floor. I wanted to know what was going to happen to me, and Blue Fox. I thought back to the information given at the meeting.

We have not yet succeeded in transferring the magic into a living life form. My son, however, proved himself worthy of being one of us. He found a magical being.

Am I the magical being? I always hit my target when I am hunting, but that is from good aim, or is it?

'When he told me this, about ten years ago, I gave him the power to change his appearance at his will. He has been bringing information to me about the being. She is one of the natives; lives in a village called Ashinders.'

I met Blue Fox ten years ago. No, Blue Fox would never in a thousand years betray me.

My son is still with her at this very moment.

No one had been in the area except me and Blue Fox, unless they were well hidden.

Blue Fox.

No, I refused to believe that Blue Fox was a traitor. He was so kind; he was not a—

"Hazel?" The voice pulled me out of my thoughts. "Hazel?" Blue Fox's eyes peered into my cell. The dimly lit hallway made his face look eerie.

"Blue Fox!" I exclaimed. "Are you okay? Who escorted you down here? Are you hurt? Is Redskin?"

"Shh," Blue Fox said quietly, "I will explain everything, but you must promise to do three things: you won't get mad, you will believe me, and you will not interrupt me until I am finished talking."

I listened to his directions and when he finished them, I nodded.

"Okay." He waved his hand and the stone bars of my cell sunk into the ground; like they did for the demons. When Blue Fox stepped inside my cell, the bars replaced themselves. He sat down beside me on the cold, hard floor. During all of this, I stared at him with fear and amusement.

Before Blue Fox began, I asked, "Is Red Wolf your real father?"

Blue Fox took a deep breath in before answering. "No, but you must understand."

"I know I said I would not interrupt, but I need to know."

"I understand."

"What about your mother? And how in Eagle Spirit's name did you manage to—"

"Let me explain." Blue Fox's voice was very grim. "Before I was born, Redskin met a beautiful native woman. Her name was Blue River. After a while, she got pregnant and had a boy who was half demon. Redskin wanted to name him Bloodriver, after his wife and his father. But Blue River wanted to give the son a proper native name, and so she decided on Blue Fox." Blue Fox looked into my eyes. "Redskin flew back to the Black Mountains and did not return until the boy was eight years old. The boy did not want to accept his parentage. He thought it was all a lie until his mother, a woman who would never lie to the boy in a thousand years, confirmed it. The boy was scared but curious to meet his father and when he did, he worshiped him. Redskin taught the boy how to shapeshift and how to fly; it was amazing."

I thought I heard Blue Fox's voice crack. I wanted to ask so many questions, but was eager to hear more of his story.

"Then one day, Redskin asked the boy to betray the boy's own friend and the boy did not want to let his father down, so he agreed to Redskin's terms. But after three years of spying on his friend, he told Redskin that he wanted no more of this. Redskin banished the boy and the only way for the boy to get back into the demon tribe was to find a worthy vessel of a powerful magic. Four years later, he did. The boy was sad and excited at the same time, but—"

A heavy door slammed shut. Blue Fox and I looked up; Blue Fox stood and walked to the bars of my cell, made them sink into the ground, and stepped into the hallway. A demon walked up to him. "Bloodriver, your father requests your presence immediately," he said.

Blue Fox nodded. "Thank you, UD4." He began to walk down the hallway then stopped. "Do we have any spare living quarters?"

The demon, UD4, spun around after realizing that Blue Fox was talking to him. He stood at attention, then said, "Redvein's room is now empty, sir. May I ask why?"

"Redvein's quarters are now Hazel's. Have them cleaned

up then bring her to them." Blue Fox began to walk down
the hall again.

"Will the chief approve? I mean we should not want
her to be happy while she is in captivity, should we, sir?"
UD4 asked.

"One thing I learned from the healers of Ashinders is that
the happier you are, the healthier you are," Blue Fox called.

"Yes *sir*." UD4 emphasized the last word and it was obvious that he was reluctant to call Blue Fox that.

After the door to the dungeon had closed again, UD4
said to me, after replacing the stone bars, "I will come get
you after the quarters have been cleaned."

Chapter 8

When UD4 came back, he did not grab my forearm and drag me to the room like Blackblood and Blueblood did; instead he waved down the bars of my cell, told me to gather all of my belongings in the cell (I had none), and simply told me to follow him to Redvein's quarters. Well, I guess they were *my* quarters now.

I have to admit, I was very tempted to bolt down one of the hallways once we were out of the dungeons.

The door to my room was just like the one to Redskin's: a large, spruce door with a bronze handle. The demon stepped into the room after unlocking the door and gestured for me to enter the room. Once I stepped over the threshold, UD4 stepped into the hallway again. Like lightning, he slammed the door shut and a split second after, I heard a loud *click*.

It took me a second to realize that the demon had locked me in the room. I hurried to the door and tried the handle. It wouldn't budge. I tried to ram the door open with my shoulder, but I ended up bruising it instead.

Exhausted, I plopped down on the couch on the left side of the room. I looked around. The quarter layout was poor and desolate: a redwood table and chair on the left, more of a bedroom on the right. A small cot had a red pillow and red sheets. There was one window that was big enough so that I could stand in it without bumping my head and its red curtains were tied open.

I walked to the window and had a great view of the valley.

I could see Ashinders, the river, and ponds that dappled the valley.

The demons' lair was built into the side of a mountain cliff; a beautiful garden lay twenty feet below my window. The garden was outlined with a green hedge and included a fountain in the center.

Sitting on a bench near the fountain was Redskin, staring into the water. Anger welled up inside me once more as Blue Fox stepped through the garden gateway. He sat down beside Redskin on the bench.

Blue Fox is a traitor. He is the reason Moonlight and Desert Flower are gone. He should be dead instead of them.

No. He shouldn't die; he *needed* to die and I would gladly be the cause. I watched as Redskin nodded at something Blue Fox had said. Blue Fox did a sort of bow, and then he turned and walked out of sight.

I stepped back from the window and stumbled on something; I looked down: it was a carpet.

When did this carpet get here?

It literally just appeared out of nowhere. I looked around the room and almost screamed. The table was emitting a faint golden glow, and the wood was slowly morphing into something else. At first, I thought it might have changed into a desk, but the wood stretched into a long table with a vase of blue snapdragons in the middle.

Blue snapdragons are my favorite type of flower.

I now turned my attention to the chair, which was also

glowing. But before it morphed, it split right down the middle, like a thousand degree dagger had cut it. The two halves morphed in sync: first, they grew two more wooden legs, then they stretched out to almost the length of the table. After that, two red velvet arms sprouted on the sides and *BAM!* Before my eyes were two couches parallel to each other; the table between them.

Now the cot, too, was glowing. Each of its four corners grew about two more feet in height. The cot thickened, and transformed into a Victorian canopy bed. I was surprised at what had just happened, but more curious as to *how* it had happened. I sat down on the squishy bed; my back to the door.

> *Well, I suppose I had been wishing that I had more comfortable quarters, but how had I done it? If I had done it.*

But before I could ponder more, someone knocked on the door. I was going to get up and open the door, but two things stopped me: I remembered that the door was locked from the outside, and "Hazel? Can I come in?" was spoken by an all too familiar voice: Blue Fox's.

I did not answer. I heard Blue Fox unlock the door and come into the room, closing it behind him.

"Hazel, I can explain everything."

"Get out please!" my voice cracked. I was, again, resisting tears. Grrr, I hated crying in front of people.

"Hazel!"

"Get out!" I demanded.

"No Hazel!" His voice was unusually stern. "You are going to hear me out, if not willingly, then I will force you to listen."

"I don't want to hear ANYTHING you have to say unless it is an apology, *Bloodriver*," I spat.

"Please don't call me that, I—"

"—am ashamed of the name? Of your parentage? Of betraying your friends? Or maybe?"

"SHUT IT AND LISTEN!" Blue Fox screamed.

I reluctantly turned around on the bed and stared daggers at Blue Fox. He had sat down on one of the couches and had a cup of steaming tea in his hand.

Where did he get the tea?

"It was the only way for me to prove myself to my father and I didn't think I would become so attached to you. I thought I would spend ten years living in Ashinders as Blue Fox then be done with it. I didn't expect to make friends." He took a sip out of his teacup and then set it down on the coffee table.

"Once we became friends, I wanted to forget that I ever made the deal with my father, but he visited twice a month to insure that I was doing my part. I *hated*, absolutely *hated* these visits. Once my mother found out what I was up to, she was so torn as to what to do: warn Ashinders, or let me join my father. She was going to warn the elders, but then father cleared her memory of him; she forgot that he ever existed. It left my mother believing that my father—whoever she thought it was—left at my birth. It hurt Redskin to have my mother forget him, but it was that or the demons' exposure. He was and is a selfish man. After mother's memory was wiped, she remarried Red Wolf, my stepfather.

"When we were hunting in the forest the day you got caught, and the demons came, I didn't want them to get you, I truly didn't. I also—"

"Is it true? That you can change your appearance at will?" I asked.

Blue Fox started, "Hazel!"

"It's a yes or no question, *Bloodriver*," I interrupted.

"I—" Blue Fox paused and then sighed, "Yes."

"Then this," I gestured to his body. "Is not your real self?"

Bloodriver shook his head.

"Show me," I demanded.

Bloodriver stood up and began to emit a red glow. Two bumps grew from his shoulder blades; it looked like hills were sprouting vertically from his back. The bottom half of the bumps folded out and then extended about two feet; so did the top half.

It was not long before Bloodriver had two five-foot wings sprouting out of his back. Next, two little horns popped out of his head two inches above his ears.

He made a t-shape with his arms and turned around slowly. During all of this, my mouth was open with amusement and disbelief.

> *How could he hide all of this from me; and for ten years, too!*

"Will this suffice?" he asked as he sat down on the couch; folding his wings in as he did.

"Is that all you have been hiding, or is there more?" I interrogated.

"This is all," Bloodriver said calmly.

I got off of the bed and hesitantly walked over to the couches. I sat down next to Bloodriver and we stared at each other for a moment.

He broke the silence. "Here, have some tea." As he said this, he cupped his hand and a full teacup appeared in it.

I took the warm cup into my hands and drank. An idea came to mind; it was a cruel one, but it had a chance of getting me out of here. I looked into Bloodriver's eyes.

"I am truly sorry about this, but I have to get out of this wretched place," I said.

Bloodriver started, "What do—"

Before he could finish, I smashed the teacup on his head, knocking him unconscious. He fell sideways onto the couch. I bolted for the door, relieved to see that it was unlocked, and ran into the hallway.

The door to my quarters did not have a keyhole, but a massive bolt.

> *When Bloodriver awakes and sees that I am gone, he will alert the other demons. I have to give myself as much time as possible.*

I bolted the door shut, locking Bloodriver in, and sped down the hallway, determined to escape.

Chapter 9

My feet carried me as fast as they could. The hallway went a long time without turns or bends. I eventually reached a fork in the hallway; the left went down a long way, the right ended at a metal door with a small, circular window near the top. In hindsight, I should have gone left, but I was curious to see what was to the right.

I walked down the right hallway to the metal door. There was a bolt on it like on my door, but the bolt was unlocked. It was not easy to open; it was very heavy, but I managed to push it open. Before I went into the room, I looked behind me to see if I was being followed. The hallway was deserted.

I stepped through the door into a large chamber, larger than Redskin's quarters. In the very center of the room was a table stacked high with documents, research papers, and books. Behind the stacks was a pile of blank paper and a quill in an ink jar. A vacant chair was sitting up on the floor next to the table.

A single door stood on the other side of the room. It was a big heavy metal door, like the entrance, but this door gave off a certain feel to it; I don't know how to describe it, it was not a *good* feeling, and *scary* didn't cut it. *Terrifying* was closer, but again, I should have stayed where I was or left the room and gone down the left hallway, but the door drew me in; I couldn't resist, like an insect being lured into a Venus flytrap.

I approached the door with caution and excitement, grabbed the handle, and pushed. It wouldn't budge. I tried again. Still no luck. In frustration, I shook the handle vertically and I almost lost my balance when the door opened towards me. Once I got over my shock, I noticed a brass sign on the door:

POSSESSION CHAMBER: BE CAREFUL WHEN USING! P.S. PULL DOOR HANDLE TO OPEN

I felt so stupid! How could I have not noticed a sign that big and that shiny? After I finished feeling idiotic, I stepped inside of the room. What I saw inside the Possession Chamber will leave a permanent mark on my brain. The chamber was half the size of the larger room, but that was not what stunned me.

Three lifeless bodies lay scattered across the floor. I recognized Red Robin's body, his dark brown hair plastered to his ghostly white face; his glassy brown eyes staring at the ceiling. Next to him, a little girl lay in the dust. Tears had drawn lines in her dusty face, and a stone was clutched in her hand, close to her chest.

I gasped. "No, no, no, no, no! No!" I kneeled next to Moonlight's body, tears streaming down my face. My sister, my precious sister, was— *No. There is still hope.*

I slowly lowered my head to Moonlight's chest and pressed my ear against it. No heartbeat. *No heartbeat.* I checked again to make sure that I was hearing correctly. There was still no *thump thump, thump thump.* This could not be happening. I could not let my sister go. I wrapped my arms around her body and pulled it into my lap. I brought her forehead up to mine and kissed it. Moonlight's vacant hazel eyes were still open and looking into mine.

With my pointer and middle finger, I closed her eyes and

tucked a piece of stray brown hair behind her ear. I buried my face in her shoulder and cried into it until her shirt was soaked with tears. I could not believe that she was gone. Forever.

I heard a shallow breathing coming from somewhere else in the room. I looked hopefully at Moonlight. Her chest was still motionless. I looked around the room. Red Robin and another older Native man lay motionless as well, their chests unmoving. The breathing seemed to be coming from a person hidden in the shadows of a wall.

I recognized the dark caramel hair and the blue bead necklace. It was Desert Flower. I scrambled over to Desert Flower and when I reached her body, pulled her out of the shadows. I had so many questions.

"Desert Flower! What happened? I thought you were dead! Everyone thought—"

"Shh, shh, shh!" Desert Flower was so quiet, I could hardly hear her. "They will hear you!"

"But!"

"Let me explain." She took a deep breath in. "Hazel, you must run. I do not want you to end up like me."

"But what happened to you?" I sobbed. I *could not* lose Desert Flower and Moonlight.

"Everyone in this room was used as an attempted vessel for a magical force. The demons intend to use you next."

"Why?"

"I believe that Redskin wants this force to himself, but he cannot put it inside of himself directly or it will kill him. By putting the magic inside of another living being, it dilutes the possibility that Redskin will perish when he takes the magic out of the being.

"Basically, Redskin has attempted to use us as a 'storage container' for the magic; he can take however much as he wants from the vessel whenever he wants. The problem is that the possibility of death is diluted for the next user, not the next vessel; the vessel actually absorbs the 'bad' magic. It weakens the vessel until they can no longer stand it; they die."

Desert Flower took a sharp inhale and a couple of shallow breaths. "Hazelnut, you must run. There is nothing that you can do for me; my time is up."

I pulled her into my lap and tears dripped off of my face and onto hers. "You can't leave me. Not after Moonlight did," I whispered.

"I do not want to, Hazel, but Eagle Spirit had these things happen for a reason and I—"

"I no longer care about what Eagle Spirit did and why! I just want people to stop dying! I want my family to stay together. First Father leaves, then Bloodriver betrays me, then Moonlight and now you!" I screamed. I didn't care if the demons came and put a deathly magical force inside of me, I just wanted to have a complete family for once.

I brought Desert Flower's face up to mine and whispered, "Please stay here. Don't die."

I rocked back and forth with Desert Flower in my lap. Suddenly, a golden light appeared around Desert Flower, lighting up the Possession Chamber. I screamed, pushed her out of my lap, and backed away from her. I could make out her face: her eyelids were closed and her face was peaceful.

The light was not doing anything to Desert Flower, and that made me curious. I waited for the light to die down and go away before crawling over to Desert Flower.

"Desert Flower," I said. "Desert Flower!" I put my hands on Desert Flower's shoulders and shook her. "No, no, no. Come back, Desert Flower, come on! You can't leave me!" I screamed a little too loudly.

"For Eagle Spirit's sake, can you shut it? I am trying to rest." The words came out of Desert Flower's mouth. "Yeah, I am still alive and well, thank you very much. I just recovered from being possessed, so I am very drained."

"How?" I said, astonished. "You were about to die, and I wished you not to, and now you are alive! Am I magic?"

"Did you ever do something that you couldn't explain? Something, well, *magical?*" Desert Flower asked as she propped herself up against a wall.

I remembered the furniture in my room morphing. "Well, kind of."

"Then you're magical! Congra—"

The door to the chamber flung open. In the doorway stood Bloodriver, Blueblood, and Redskin. All of them looked very angry. I slowly pulled Desert Flower back into my lap; she, too, had a look of fear on her face.

"Please," I begged the demons. "Don't hurt Desert Flower. She did not do anything to you. She deserves to be back in Ashinders."

Redskin grimaced. "Well, now you are both going to—ARGH!"

Desert Flower was again glowing, but this time, the light seemed to be *under* her skin. She held up her hand and stared at it, then looked at me. "You just wished me back to Ashinders, Hazel. I am going home." Her hand had started to evaporate. "Hazel, wish yourself home, then we can all be free." Her legs had started to evaporate, too.

"I wish Moonlight's body to go home. Have a proper burial for her and tell Mother that I love her." I smiled at Desert Flower. We both looked at Moonlight's body; it had also begun to glow and evaporate. "I wish myself home." My skin, too began to glow, but it did not evaporate. The glow was dimming.

What is happening?

I looked over to Redskin. His hand was extended and emitting a red glow. He was canceling out my magic.

All that remained of Desert Flower now was her neck and head. "What is happening? Hazel!"

"I will be alright." Tears were gushing down my cheeks. "You are safe. That is the important thing."

Desert Flower's face disappeared and Blueblood sent tendrils of thick black rope around my torso and limbs. Desert Flower was safe. Moonlight was dead. I was going to die.

Chapter 10

After Blueblood brought me back to my quarters, Redskin stationed a guard at my door that only allowed visitors if they had permission from Redskin.

I had the same meal three times a day, like when I was in the cell, but these meals were much nicer, cooked quail, roasted potatoes, a cup of milk, and occasionally a bowl of warm squash soup.

I spent at least another week in my room with nothing to do except look out the window, sleep, eat, and be bored. The only time I got to leave the room (with three "escorts") was when a strange man called Dr. Peterston took a sample of my blood. Peterston obviously wasn't a Native, for his skin was white. I suspected that he came from the City. He stuck a long needle up my arm and drew a *lot* of blood. It hurt terribly, and when I asked for something to relieve the pain, Redskin ordered the demons to put me back in my room.

Redskin was a very mysterious man, as were all of the demons, but I never got to ask about his past. It was all quite annoying, really.

Redskin also put a stiff leather band around my wrist, which apparently disabled my magic. Bloodriver visited once, but I attempted to kill him with a writing quill.

I SAT ON THE windowsill and watched a mother cardinal fly to her nest in a tall maple tree where three hungry chicks sat waiting for breakfast. The mother dropped a worm into each of the chicks' mouths, then gobbled down a worm herself. The mother bird then flew off into the forest to find more food for her young. I wished I could fly, so I could fly right out of the window and be free; free of my despair and of that prison.

I heard the bolt screech open and looked at the door. A demon stepped into my room carrying my breakfast.

"Set it on the table," I told the demon quietly.

"Special order courtesy of Sir Bloodriver," the demon said as he closed the door and bolted it shut again.

"Special order?" I repeated to myself.

I got up from the windowsill and walked to the coffee table where my breakfast sat. I was very happy to see that instead of the usual meal (quail, potatoes, and milk), on the tray sat a steaming bowl of oatmeal, a cup of orange liquid, and a slice of warm buttered bread.

I sat down on the couch and picked up the wooden spoon off the tray and began spooning mouthfuls of oatmeal into my mouth. After I was finished with that, I ate the bread. It tasted wonderful, the airiness of the dough; the butteriness. Next, I chugged down the orange liquid; it was bitter, but at the same time sweet.

The demon had said that the meal was courtesy of Bloodriver. If that were true, why would Bloodriver be so nice to me after I tried to kill him—*twice*?

Even though Bloodriver was a demon and a traitor, he still had the same kind heart as Blue Fox. I suddenly felt a deep need to apologize to Bloodriver.

I stood up and ran to the door and banged with my fist. "Guard! I must speak to Bloodriver!" I demanded loudly.

The guard opened the door a crack and asked in a gruff voice, "Why? Last time I allowed him in you attempted to murder him."

"Funny coming from you, a murderer yourself!"

"Do not speak to me like that, young lady! I am a very

high-classed demon guard! Once a personal bodyguard of the great Demon Queen herself!"

This demon seemed awfully boastful.

"The Queen? Wow, you must have been pretty good to have guarded *her*," I said in a not very impressed, but pretending to be impressed voice.

The demon beamed. "I think I was Her Majesty's favorite."

"Oh my! Her Majesty's number one?"

"Yep, but she never admitted it; I was not the only bodyguard, so she would not say that I was her favorite in front of the other guards," boasted the demon.

"This seems like a conversation that we should have over tea. Want to come in?" I asked in a falsely sweet voice.

"I would love to; but do you have any tea or cups or anything?" the demon asked.

"Well, no; but I was hoping that, seeing as you *are* a powerful, strong demon, you could supply those for me." I was trying my best to flirt with the demon. If this guy fell for this, he was the dumbest person—er *demon*—in the valley.

"Why, I would gladly do so for such a lady!" He opened the door and stepped inside. We made ourselves comfortable on the couches and he magicked a teapot and teacups out of the air.

"...and that is why I want to get home," I finished.

The demon had been staring into my eyes dreamily but now suddenly sat up straight. "Wow! I simply cannot imagine why Chief Redskin would want to lock up such a nice lady!"

I was blushing for real. I had never heard someone talk about me that way before and this demon was just so nice.

"Would it be alright with you if I could get some fresh air and take a short walk through the halls?" I asked sweetly.

"I suppose that would be fine. No, wait!" The demon stood up abruptly and then said, "Absolutely not! I have orders not to let you out of this room and I will follow orders or—"

Before he could say another word, I picked up the teapot and smashed it over the demon's head. He went unconscious and fell to the floor, smacking his head hard on the stone. I ran to the door and bolted the demon in, and knowing that it would not hold him long, I ran down the hall thinking,

I guess I have a thing for knocking demons unconscious with teacups and teapots.

When I reached the fork in the hallway, I went left this time. This hallway had lots of forks and multidirection corners. I went straight until I came to a familiar heavy spruce door: the door to Redskin's chamber.

Chapter 11

I banged on the door with my fist. The door was opened an inch and a demon stared at me through the crack. "What is your purpose coming here?" he asked.

"I wish to speak with Bloodriver. It is urgent."

"Who are you?"

"I am Hazelnut."

"Hazel," the demon *was* Bloodriver. "When I tried to visit *you*, you tried to kill me with common household objects. I cannot imagine what would happen if I allowed you in *here*."

"Please, I promise I won't kill you. I *need* to talk to you in private."

"How did you escape?"

"I smashed a teapot over the guard's head."

"Typical," Bloodriver grinned. Now this is the Blue Fox I knew. Not *Bloodriver* the son of the demon king!

"Can I come in now?" I pestered.

"Yeah sure," he said as he opened the door wider. I stepped inside and Bloodriver closed the door. I now noticed a large window like the one I had in my quarters.

"Look," I began, "I am really sorry for trying to kill you. I should not be so mad at you; you just wanted to join your father, and I blamed you for Moonlight's death and—"

"Moonlight is dead?"

I didn't respond because Bloodriver already knew the answer before the question left his lips.

"Oh, I am so sorry, Hazel. I didn't know that."

Heavy footsteps could now be heard coming closer to the door, along with Redskin's deep voice. "How did she escape you? How could a child like her slip through *your* fingers?" he shouted.

He seemed to be right outside of the door now. I began to panic and grabbed Bloodriver's hand. "Bloodriver! What do we do?" I whispered urgently.

"I did not know that he would be here! I thought Father would be out longer. He said until Noon."

"It *is* Noon!" I said a little too loudly. Redskin had stopped yelling at the other demons. "Did you hear that?" he asked them.

He turned the doorknob and slowly opened the door. When he saw me, standing hand in hand with Bloodriver, his eyes widened in shock. He quickly extinguished the shock with a devilish grin. "How convenient! We were just heading to your quarters to pick you up for possession, but since you are here, we do not need to go all of the way back to your chamber."

Redskin signaled the demons to seize me, and two demons, Blueblood and Blackblood, came forward and grabbed my arms. This time, I thrashed and squirmed and tried to pull myself free. I most certainly did not want to be brought to the Possession Chamber to be—well—possessed.

I attempted to pull my arms free, but the demons' grip was very strong. I tried to kick both demons in the crotch, but Blackblood threatened to break my leg again if I did not stop.

I still tried to kick and pull my arms free.

The demons were inches from the door when it slammed shut. Blueblood halted and stared at the door. Blackblood stepped forward and had a go at trying to open the door, but seeing as he was sweating from the strain of trying to open it and the red glimmer on the door, it was magically sealed shut.

Blueblood raised his hand and a tiny spurt of blue smoke flared out of his hand. It was a very poor amount of magical smoke.

When the smoke floated to the floor, and the door remained shut, Blueblood turned to Bloodriver, who was staring daggers at my two escorts.

"What is the meaning of this, son?" Redskin asked Bloodriver.

"I will not let you harm her," Bloodriver said sternly.

"You will not let me harm her? What is that supposed to mean?"

"I am pretty sure that you can hear, but I will repeat myself one more time. I will not let you hurt her."

"Let me get this straight, you agreed to capture her, but will not let her be possessed?"

"Yes."

Redskin did not move for a moment, but then rose his hand with his palm facing Bloodriver and a red streak of smoke flew out of his hand, hitting Bloodriver square in the chest. He flew through the air, crashed to the ground, and skidded across the floor; stopping inches away from the windowsill.

Bloodriver tried to prop himself up against the window, but Redskin 'held' him to the floor. He walked up to Bloodriver, who was struggling greatly, bent down on one knee and put his face close to Bloodriver's. "I thought I had changed you, but there is *still* some good in you. I must extinguish it." He turned his head to look at Blueblood, then looked at Blackblood who was still trying to pry the door open.

He pulled a knife out of a sheath around his waist and pressed it against Bloodriver's neck; not stabbing him, but slowly breaking the skin.

"NO!" I screamed and attempted to pull myself free of Blueblood's grasp. "DON'T YOU DARE HURT HIM!" I cried. "That is your wife's child. Why in Eagle Spirit's name would you kill him?"

But Redskin did not seemed to have heard me and continued to press the knife into Bloodriver. "Open the door," he growled, "or the knife goes in deeper."

Bloodriver shook his head, but the red glow on the door flickered and then disappeared. Redskin saw this and smiled at Bloodriver's pained face, then looked at Blackblood, who had managed to pull the door open but lost his balance in the process and now laid sprawled out on the floor. "Take her to the Possession Chamber. I will deal with him."

I would not cooperate for these demons. "No! Please don't hurt him! He has not done anything to you, you monster! You—" Blueblood covered my mouth with his hand, muffling my insults. As I bit into his hand, he cried out in pain. He quickly brandished a bandana with his magic, and put it over my mouth. He dragged me out of Redskin's chamber and Blackblood stepped into the hall and closed the door.

I did not scream; that was useless. So was struggling. I locked my legs to try to slow Blueblood down, but he easily lifted me off of the ground.

Once we reached the fork in the hallway, I really began to panic. Blueblood carried me down the right fork of the hall and through the heavy metal door.

Dr. Peterston was sitting at his desk reading a thick book and taking notes when we walked in the room. He looked up at me struggling in Blueblood's arms and looked confused for a second. "Ah! yes!" he exclaimed.

He rose from his chair and walked over to the door to the Possession Chamber entrance. From around his neck he took a key and inserted it into a small keyhole in the middle of the door. He opened the door wide and left it open as he walked over to a small wooden door that I had not noticed before.

Before I could look behind the wooden door, Blueblood carried me into the Possession Chamber. I now noticed a set of metal cuffs chained to the wall. Blueblood had a key in his hand and used it to open the cuffs and place the cuffs around my wrists.

The cuffs had enough chain on them so that I could stand up and kick Blueblood in the crotch. I kicked at his mid-section and my foot made contact with his pelvis. Bad idea. I was chained to the wall and could not run anywhere.

Blueblood raised his hand and struck me across the face, hard. I cried out in pain.

"You foolish girl!" Blueblood cackled.

"Mr. Blueblood, I have the magic."

Blueblood and I turned our heads to look at Dr. Peterston, who was standing in the doorway of the Possession Chamber holding a large jar. Inside of the jar was a glowing orange sphere hovering in the center. It gave off turquoise flares. Beads of sweat began to trickle down my face, mixing with tears of fear.

Dr. Peterston tipped the jar toward me and the magic hovered out of the jar, inches away from my chest. Inches away from my death. Blueblood raised his hand and the magic moved an inch toward me.

"Wait!" Blackblood said. "Shouldn't we wait for Chief Redskin?"

Blueblood sighed and dropped his hand. The magic stopped. I knew my death was only postponed minutes, but I was relieved; my tense body relaxed just a little.

I heard someone scream. Blackblood looked curious and peeked out of the Possession Chamber. He stepped out of the door and allowed Redskin into the chamber.

I gasped. Redskin had a knife pressed against the neck of a thrashing Bloodriver. One arm was looped under Bloodriver's arm, the other holding a familiar silver knife just under Bloodriver's jaw.

The scream had been emitted by Bloodriver, who continued to shout, "Do not hurt her! Please! Use me instead!"

"You'll be next," Redskin snarled.

"I cannot believe that I trusted you! You are a monster! How could Mother have ever loved you?"

That made the smirk on Redskin's face slide off. He took a deep inhale, and said, "Blueblood, continue." Bloodriver squirmed more, but Redskin held fast.

My heart began to speed up again and my body began to tense. The magic moved toward me again. I tried to break the chains, but it was futile. I could feel the magic against my skin and looked down at my chest. The magic was going into my body. I could feel it; it felt like ice, yet it burned at the same time.

The magic was almost completely inside of me when a wave of lethargy swept over me. I felt the desire to close my eyes and sleep. But I couldn't; I would never wake again.

I can honestly say that I tried to keep my eyes open, but eventually, my muscles shut down and my eyes closed. I could flutter them open, but only for seconds.

As my eyes closed for the final time, I saw Bloodriver shake off Redskin and run toward me. He pulled my dying self into his lap and cradled me as I had done with Moonlight, his tears dripping onto my face. I gave him a weak smile and tried to bring my hand up to his cheek, but my muscles were weak. My hand fell to my side and my eyelids shut.

Chapter 12

My eyes flickered open.

I was alive? No. That would be impossible. The magic went into me.

I looked around. I was still in the Possession Chamber, in Bloodriver's lap. He was crying, "Hazel, don't fall asleep. Stay with me, Hazel, stay with me."

I sat up so I could look around more easily. Everything was how it had been before I passed into unconsciousness. Redskin, Blueblood, Blackblood, and Dr. Peterston all stood in the chamber staring at me. I turned to face Bloodriver, who was still crying.

"Bloodriver, I'm right here." He didn't seem to have heard.

"Bloodriver," I said a little louder. He still paid no attention to me. I was getting a bit irritated with him. He was staring into his lap. I looked at his lap and tried to maintain a calm mood, but let out a small gasp. I blinked a couple of times to make sure I was seeing right.

In Bloodriver's lap lay me. My body lay limp and lifeless, eyes shut, with a weak smile on my face. I raised my hand to observe it. It was ghostly white and translucent; so was my arm, my shoulder, and my dress. My whole body was translucent and white.

I reached out to touch Bloodriver's cheek, but when my fingers should have made contact with his face, they went right through it.

"What in the name of Eagle Spirit is going on?" I asked weakly. Then I remembered no one could hear me.

I stood up and observed the other demons. Blueblood and Blackblood both had their arms folded against their chest and had a small grin on their face; Redskin looked slightly disappointed.

I had an idea that brought a small smile across my face. I walked over to where Redskin stood, cocked my fist, and threw it into Redskin's face. Again. My fist went through his face.

So, no one can hear me, see me, or feel me. I cannot touch anyone. So that makes me a ghost! But if I am dead, and this is the afterlife, where is my perished family?

"Family?" I said aloud. I though about Mother and Ocean Lotus, who both thought I would come back to the shack that day, having no idea where I was. I needed to see if they were okay.

The Possession Chamber around me began to grow faint; the demons' faces, Dr. Peterston, the chamber walls, and all. Everything was fading to white. I felt a jolt behind my navel and suddenly was standing in the living room of my house. My mother was sitting on the buffalo skin couch, her head in her hands. Her brown hair was in a loose, messy bun and her shoulders were shaking. She was crying.

I looked down at the floor in front of Mother and there laid Moonlight's body. Her eyes were closed, just as mine were, and there was a water stain on Moonlight's shoulder where I had cried.

Desert Flower was on her knees near Moonlight's head, silent tears running down her face. Ocean Lotus was standing behind Mother with her hands on Mother's shoulders. She, too, was weeping soundless tears of grief.

I was also beginning to weep; the scene was so depressing. I walked over to the couch and sat down next to my mother. I was going to put my arm around her, as I was a ghost; I could not touch anyone.

For a long time, we just sat there weeping over Moonlight's dead body.

KNOCK KNOCK.

All four of us looked up at the door. No one rose to open it, they just stared, too sad to answer. Finally, Ocean Lotus moved from behind the couch and to the threshold.

She turned the knob and opened the door to reveal a middle aged man with short, brown hair, a skinny build, and a black beaded necklace. He wore a large leather tunic that was almost too big for him, as were the moccasins he wore on his feet. But this man was in a disguise. The only thing that gave this away was the red glow of the man's eyes. A glow that was all too familiar. This man was Redskin.

"Is this the house of Nightingale?" he inquired.

"Um—y-yes." Ocean Lotus stepped away from the door as Mother approached it.

"I regret to inform you that your daughter, Hazelnut, has died." He took a quick glance at Moonlight's body laying on the floor. "I understand that you are in a deep state of grief, but I was told to deliver this information to you immediately. Good day to you, all of you."

"To you as well," Mother said, almost whispering as she closed the door ever so slowly. Once the door clicked shut, Mother fell to the floor sobbing. This time, it was not silent.

Desert Flower was staring, wide-eyed, at the door. Her tears had stopped; they had made clean streaks across her dirty face. "I knew it," she whispered to herself.

Ocean Lotus and Mother looked at Desert Flower. "Knew what?" Mother asked.

"That she would die."

"How did you know?"

"The demons had her and she took my place. I was almost dead."

Mother's tears had stopped too. She looked more angry than sad now. "She took your place? Willingly?"

"Yes."

Mother stood up. "It's not fair!"

"What?" Desert Flower questioned.

Mother was furious. She looked at Desert Flower. "It's not fair that she died, yet you lived! You should have died! I would prefer to cry over you than to cry over Hazel! No one would miss you except for Hazel! You have no parents, no family! NO ONE CARES ABOUT YOU!" She started crying again. "Everyone cares about Hazelnut. I cared."

I was so shocked at my mother's words. I knew her as a kind, loving person. I never expected her to yell at someone and criticize them. Especially Desert Flower.

"Hazelnut," said someone's voice. A woman's voice.

I looked around the room and saw a woman standing behind my mother. She was beautiful.

Her skin was olive, her brown hair pulled back into a braid, her caramel eyes were warming. She wore a white tunic and she seemed to glow.

"Hazelnut," she said again.

"Who are you? What do you want?" I said a bit too defensively.

"I am Rose Petal, Eagle Spirit's wife. I wanted to see your

reactions to these events." She gestured to the argument in front of us. "You know who that man was, correct?"

"Redskin."

"Yes, now watch." We both turned to watch the argument. Mother was in the same position she had been before: standing in front of the door. Desert Flower was now standing up, fists clenched, and eyebrows furrowed. She looked as if she were literally about to explode.

Ocean Lotus had dragged Moonlight's body under the dining table and was cradling it like a mother would her infant.

I listened to Mother yell at Desert Flower, "You are worthless to this tribe!" I wanted to yell at Mother that I was here, but number one, I couldn't, I was a ghost; and number two, I wasn't exactly *there*. All I could do was watch Mother yell insults at Desert Flower until Desert Flower finally blew.

"It's not my fault that Hazel died! Do you think I wanted her to? Do you think I wanted Moonlight to die, either? NO! I wish my parents were still alive, that the viper's nest hadn't been where it was that day! But it was! It's not like I can change the past, as much as I wish I could, BUT I CAN'T! I CAN'T!"

"I am not stupid, I know you cannot. You could have at least protested before she 'magicked' you out of the chamber!" Mother seemed to mock the word 'magic'.

"I told you, she was going to 'magic' herself out, but the lead demon disabled her magic! I was already evaporating."

"WELL YOU SHOULD HAVE—"

Cough.

Everyone, including me and Rose Petal, turned to look at Ocean Lotus, who had stood up from under the table and seemed to be the one to have emitted the cough.

"It is almost Noon. Desert Flower, will you be staying for tea? I will also be making sourdough bread." Her nervous face indicated that interrupting this fight was dangerous by her standards.

Both Desert Flower and Mother looked shocked at this interruption. "Er—yes, I think I will."

"Excellent!" Ocean Lotus walked over to the stove and began to boil water in a tea kettle. When she stole an anxious glance at Mother and Desert Flower and saw that they were still staring daggers at each other, she said cheerily, "Desert Flower, would you mind helping me with the bread dough?"

Desert Flower dropped her deathly stare and walked over to the kitchen to start the bread dough. Mother sighed, looked at Moonlight's body, and said gloomily, "I am sorry, Desert Flower. I am just upset at Hazel's death, for I am alone now."

Desert Flower's face became less tense when she said, "It's alright, I understand."

"I am going to take a nap. Wake me when you are finished with the food."

As Mother was walking to her room, Desert Flower said into the mixing bowl, "You are not alone."

Then the house around me started to become translucent, so did Rose Petal, her figure fading away, and in a moment, I was standing over nothing, a pit of darkness, and I fell into oblivion.

Chapter 13

My feet came in contact with a hard surface and the sudden impact made me collapse. I blinked my eyes open and was almost blinded by the whiteness of my surroundings.

When my eyes finally adjusted, I saw that I was in a long hallway. It had white walls, a white ceiling, white floors, white everything except the occasional pot of red roses on a marble pedestal. Rose Petal stood further down the hall, back turned, talking to a man with slicked back brown hair and dark brown skin, but piercing blue eyes. He, too, was completely dressed in white. Both beings seemed to literally glow.

The man saw me, smiled, and walked toward me. I avoided making eye contact by looking down at my chest. I was dressed in white as well: a white silk shirt and pants, my feet were bare. As the man approached me, my tense body relaxed and I felt comforted. "Hazelnut, daughter of Nightingale and Tufted Deer, come here."

I cautiously stood up and walked over to the man; I still didn't know who he was, but I had a faint idea. "Eagle Spirit?"

"Yes. Come, let us walk." His voice echoed across the long hallway. I began to walk alongside him down the hallway. Rose Petal had disappeared.

"Where is Rose Petal?" I asked.

"Gone to fetch a visitor."

"For me?"

"Perhaps." A small smile slowly spread across Eagle Spirit's face.

"Eagle Spirit?"

"Hmm?"

"Am I dead?"

"You, my child, are neither dead or alive. This is my palace, as you may have guessed. You are a lost soul. You think you are dead and you do not know the impact your life had on others, but I suspect that you got a glimpse of that when Rose Petal showed you your mother."

"Is there a way to get back?"

"To your body?"

"Yes."

"There is. Once in awhile, when a soul is very lost, I give it a second chance. You are most definitely a lost soul. But enough talk, let us see this visitor."

When we had arrived at a white door, Eagle Spirit turned the knob and we stepped inside of the room. Unlike the rest of the palace, the visiting room was black. The space was square and along the walls were wooden benches. Rose Petal was standing in the middle of the room, literally lighting it up. Her head bowed and her hands were interlaced. "I ask you now to bring her spirit to us without any disturbance."

Eagle Spirit shut the door after I had entered the room, leaving me and Rose Petal in the visiting room alone. Rose Petal had finished her prayer and now looked up at me. "She will be here momentarily. I'll be waiting outside the door when you are finished."

I was confused and had many questions. "Who is 'she'? Why are you leaving? What is this place?"

"All will be explained," she said as she closed the door, allowing the darkness to swallow me.

I could feel my heart beating, *THUMP THUMP.* What

was going to happen? I knew I couldn't die; I was already dead. I was just extremely scared.

Suddenly, the wall opposite of the door began to emit a blue glow that lit up the whole room. The light made me feel surprisingly comfortable. A glowing figure emerged from the wall. At first, I couldn't make out its limbs or features, then, the light formed into a little girl with brown eyes, black hair, and a round, chubby face. Her body floated inches above the ground and emitted a blue glow. I recognized her face, her leather tunic, the heartwarming smile.

"Moonlight," I gasped.

She smiled and nodded. I couldn't believe it! My sister, Moonlight, was here! My eyes began to fill with tears of joy.

"Moonlight! I can't believe you're here!" I cried. I expected her to laugh and float over to me, embrace me and kiss me on the cheek just as she had done when she was alive, but she stayed stationary while simply smiling and nodding.

"Can, can you hear me?"

Moonlight nodded.

"Can you speak to me?"

Another nod.

"Then how come you are not speaking to me now?"

Moonlight sighed, "Well, you didn't always talk when I wanted you to, so why should I?"

My spirits lifted slightly and a big, fat smile spread across my face.

"Are you okay? Where have you been? Why—"

"Just be quiet. Come, sit." She floated down and sat down on one of the benches, then patted next to her, indicating for me to join her. I walked over and did so. It was strange to be sitting next to my dead sister, her glowing face smiling at me.

"Rose Petal found me a few days ago in the Void."

"What's the Void?"

"Where souls go until Eagle Spirit or Rose Petal personally retrieves them to place them in their palace. Every soul gets its own room in the palace. Anyway," Moonlight said dramatically, "after Rose Petal found me, she brought me to my room. She supplied me with more food than I could eat."

"So, you *are* dead."

"Yes."

"Then, if you are dead, where is Father?"

"I think he did as he said he would. He came back as a stag. You should ask Rose Petal."

"Okay," I sighed in disappointment. I was hoping that Father would just appear, like Moonlight did. It felt so good to see my sister, and I bet it would feel great to see Father too.

"Moony?" I asked.

"Hmm?" Moonlight replied dreamily.

"I've missed you more than anything this past month. I feel like I truly have no family anymore."

"What about Mother, Ocean Lotus, and," she took a dramatic pause, "Blue Fox." She said his name in a high-pitched, teasing voice. She always teased me about liking Blue Fox, even though we were just friends.

Blue Fox. I have not heard that name in a long time. Did Moony not know that he was the reason I was dead? That he was a traitor and a liar? If she was still referring to Bloodriver as 'Blue Fox', then most certainly not.

"Moony, I need to tell you something."

Suddenly, Moonlight jumped on me and hugged me tight. She didn't go through me, which was weird considering she was translucent and ghostly.

"Oh Hazel! I just knew that it would happen! I knew it, I knew it, I KNEW IT!" she screamed excitedly.

I looked down at her smiling face, confused. "Knew what?"

"That you and Blue Fox were going to get married!" she squealed.

"Um," I didn't know how to respond to this. Should I tell Moony the truth? Or lie to her and keep this happy moment safe?

"Moonlight," I pulled her off of me and held her shoulders tight. "Blue Fox is a demon. He betrayed me and you. He is a liar and a thief; I would never marry such a person."

For a moment Moonlight stared at me like I was an alien, then she burst out laughing, clutching her stomach. "Oh Hazelnut! My death must have changed your mentality level!" she laughed. "Blue Fox would never do that in a million years; he is so nice! What did he do to make you jealous?"

"What? No." I was growing more and more upset with Moonlight for not believing me. "Moonlight, I am serious! He really is a traitor and a—"

"Hazel, Hazel, Hazel!" She was laughing so hard that she was crying. "If Blue Fox is a demon, then I'm a," she took a deep, shaky breath, "then I'm a flying monkey!" She burst into a fit of laughter again, and this time, fell to the floor with a *thud*.

I didn't think ghosts could fall onto the floor with a *thud*.

"Moonlight, this is a serious matter and is not to be laughed at! You must believe that I speak wholeheartedly!"

For some reason, that made Moonlight laugh even harder. "Oh, now you sound like Mother! Would you like me to go fetch water from the river?"

It was futile to attempt to reason with my sister I found out. I gave up and put my head in my hands. Moonlight's laughter died down after a couple of minutes, and after that it was just silence. I did not weep, but I was just about to begin to when I felt Moonlight's hand on my shoulder.

"Hazel, I'm sorry, but I just think it's absurd that Blue Fox would betray us. Now, I only have two minutes left, so if there is anything else that you want to say to me, do it now." Her voice sounded serious.

I looked up into Moonlight's big brown eyes and sighed, "Oh, I just wish that you could come back with me."

"I am."

"You are?"

"Yes. Not in this form, but I *am* coming back."

"What form, then, if not this form?"

"A red-tailed fox."

"Nice."

The room suddenly flooded with light and Rose Petal walked in. "Moonlight, it's time to go."

Moonlight looked at Rose Petal sadly and nodded. Rose Petal smiled and reached out her hands to my sister. Moonlight looked back at me, smiling, and hugged me tight. I closed my eyes and hugged back.

All of my worries were abruptly wiped away, and I was glad for that. I was never going to see her and recognize her immediately again. "I love you," I whispered into Moony's ear.

"I love you too," she said.

Moonlight pulled away from the hug and the worry-free serenity went away in a poof.

She walked toward the door, hand in hand with Rose Petal, but then suddenly stopped. "Rose Petal, can't Hazelnut just go back with me? She is going back anyway."

"Well," I could tell Rose Petal was becoming a victim of Moony's inevitable puppy eyes. "Why not? Eagle Spirit is probably watching the mortals again, but we must be quiet."

I stood up and merrily trotted over to where the duo stood. Rose Petal led us out of the visiting room and quietly down the hall. We reached the end of the hall which opened into a large chamber, not like the Possession Chamber; this new chamber's walls were completely made of glass. On the floor, there was a large, blue circle. It radiated power, but it was not frightening.

Rose Petal guided us to the center of the circle, where Moonlight and I stood holding hands. I grinned down at her happy face and she smiled back.

"Moonlight," came Rose Petal's voice, "when you reach the mortal world, you will find your father in a cave near the Great Waterfall. He knows that you are coming. I contacted him while you were in the visiting room."

"Alright. What about Hazelnut?" Moony asked sweetly.

"Hazelnut," Rose Petal turned to me, "once *you* reach the mortal world, the demons will not expect you, so you must take the time that they are surprised to escape. I have rearranged some things so that when you wake, you will not be in chains."

I bowed low to her. "Thank you, Rose Petal." She bowed back. Rose Petal raised her hands and the blue circle began to glow. The last thing that I saw before I woke up in the Possession Chamber was Eagle Spirit's wife's smiling face, then everything disappeared in a blue flash.

Chapter 14

My eyelids flew open as quick as lightning. I was still in the Possession Chamber with Redskin, Blueblood, Blackblood, and Bloodriver, who was still cradling me. None of them seemed to know that I was awake yet: Bloodriver was crying with his eyes closed while Redskin was deep in conversation with Blueblood and Blackblood.

I took a deep breath in, which made Bloodriver open his eyes and stare at me in amusement. He didn't say anything, which, in a way, was kind of fortunate. I smiled up at Bloodriver and began to prop myself up when Blackblood spotted me out of the corner of his eye. "She's alive!" he shrieked.

Redskin and Blueblood looked at me with wide eyes. Redskin saw that I was no longer in chains and ran toward me screaming, "Seize her!"

I forgot about what Rose Petal had said:

Take the time that they are surprised to escape.

I panicked instead. Redskin was inches away from me when Bloodriver raised his hand and sent his father flying across the room and through the doorway. If I hadn't been scared out of my mind that Redskin might kill me, I would have laughed.

Redskin was as angry as the fires of Hell. He stormed

back into the room and magically cast Bloodriver into the opposite wall. Like actually *into* the wall. I watched in horror as Bloodriver went through layers and layers of rock until his figure became swallowed by the darkness.

I turned my attention back to Redskin, who was walking toward me again.

> *Please don't kill me. Please don't kill me. Please don't kill me.*

He reached out to grab my arm, but an electric blue sphere erupted around me and Redskin went flying out of the Possession Chamber again. This time I laughed.

Blueblood and Blackblood were still standing there, unharmed and prepared to fight. They advanced toward me just as Redskin had done, and received the same treatment. All three demons laid stunned in a heap just outside of the door. Dr. Peterston stood at the head of the pile, confused. "What is going—" He saw me sitting on the floor, staring up at him. "YOU'RE ALIVE?"

"Very much, thank you," I added as I stood up.

Dr. Peterston nodded and cautiously backed away from the demon pile. I walked through the chamber door and stepped over the pile. Once I reached the heavy metal door that led out to the labyrinth hallways, I turned to Dr. Peterston. "Once they recover, tell them that I've gone to Redskin's chamber." He nodded.

"Oh, how do I get out of the mountain?" I asked him.

"Take the left hallway then two rights and a left," he answered merrily.

"Two rights and a left. Got it! Thank you so much Doctor," I called as I exited the Possession Chamber, hopefully for the last time.

I took the left hallway as Peterston had directed, then

walked down the hall a long time before reaching the first right. It was then that I began to suspect that Dr. Peterston had lied to me. The hallway continued straight, well lit and welcoming, and the right hall was dimly lit. I hesitated before continuing down the right hallway.

Dr. Peterston would never lie to me. He is also a captive of the demons; I should have brought him with me. No. He is a kind man and would never lie.

I took another right. The only thing that I could hear was my moccasins *thump thumping* on the stone floor and my breath.

My legs began to tire; this hall seemed to never end. I was about to give up, turn around, and attempt to find my way back to the Possession Chamber, when I saw a light at the end of the tunnel; literally. Ahead, a white light was coming from the left turn. I sighed in relief; I wasn't lost, Peterston didn't lie to me. I sprinted down the hallway and turned left. The next thing I saw made me so happy that I could have cried.

The left turn didn't lead to another hallway, but a cave. The mouth of the cave overlooked the whole valley in which lay Ashinders, the river, the Black Mountains, and the other villages. I spotted the river, which began near the Black Mountains, ran through the Great Plains, the woods, and finally ended in a big waterfall that pooled into a lake a couple miles south of Ashinders.

I could just make out Ashinders, its bright red market canopies, the line of oak shacks, the smoke rising from the chimney of the elders' home. I took a deep, relaxed inhale. I was almost home, and nothing was going to stop me. Well, except for the three hundred feet between me and the ground; the cave was built into the side of the mountain.

I approached the mouth of the cave and cautiously looked over the edge. "Oh Eagle Spirit help me," I muttered. The drop was way more terrifying than I expected. Directly vertical from where I stood, I could hear the river raging. It ran so fast, it could have dragged someone under within the blink of an eye.

The only way to get down was to climb. *Or to fly,* I thought as I stared at Ashinders again. Then it hit me.

"I am so stupid!" I exclaimed, then slapped my hand to my mouth, fearing the demons would hear me.

> *This was the place where they take off to demolish people's lives.*

I glanced back down at the rushing river. "I need to get home to my family."

There was a small foothold a couple of feet down from the ledge of the cave. I sat down on the floor, my feet dangling over the edge, and slid my foot into the niche.

"Okay, okay, I got this, Rose Petal," I exhaled as I lowered my whole body off of the ledge. "Okay. I-I can do this," I whimpered. I was committed now, there was no turning back. I fit my foot into another pocket in the mountainside and used the previous foothold for my hand.

I sighed in relief; I had made it down the first five feet, now I just had to make it down the other 295. I looked around for other footholds or handholds, but I saw none. There was a little ledge about five feet down from where I was, but if I tried to jump down, there was a possibility that I could miss or hurt myself.

> *Well, I can't exactly go back up, and the only way to get further down is to try to jump to that ledge.*

I inhaled deeply, then whispered to myself, "You can do this." I exhaled and pulled my foot free of the rock pocket. Now, the only thing that kept me from falling was my left hand, which was loosely holding onto another pocket. The sharp rock was cutting into my palm and fingers; I had to let go soon.

I closed my eyes and took some deep breaths in and out. "Rose Petal and Eagle Spirit," I muttered, "please forgive me for my wrongdoing and allow me to get home safely to my family and all who need me in Ashinders. Amen."

I stared down at the ledge, preparing myself for whatever came next. I could feel the rock pocket slicing my fingers and the warm blood trickling down my hand. I took one last breath before I released my grip on the pocket and fell through the air.

My feet hit the rocky ledge a moment later. My breath fast and shallow, I looked down and sighed in relief; even though the ledge was barely big enough to cover the diameter of my feet, I had landed on it and not fallen to my death.

"Okay, Hazelnut, just breathe," I murmured.

Slowly and carefully, I looked at the mountain surface below, hopeful to see rock pockets and footholds crammed all together. But the mountain was as smooth as a sanded stone, there were no pockets in sight. The smooth surface ran for at least 100 feet, for that was where the mountain became engulfed in fog.

Well, I could slide down and hope that there is a platform there, but if nothing is there, then I would fall down the mountain and into the river. Then I would drown, and that would—Crack!

I looked at the rock ledge. "Oh my gods," I whimpered. The little rock ledge was breaking off from the mountainside. I guess I was going down the mountain either way.

I slowly began to kneel down onto the little ledge. *Crack! Crack!* If there was a ledge there, then Eagle Spirit has heard my prayers. *Crack! Crack!* If there was nothing, then I would be with Rose Petal once more. *Crack!* Tiny fragments of rock tumbled down the mountain into the blanket of fog.

With a final booming *crack!,* the little rock ledge broke free of the mountainside. For a moment, I kept my balance and 'surfed' down the mountain's smooth surface using the rock as a board. But when the rock went over a bump, I lost my balance and fell onto my butt. It was at this point that I slid into the blanket of fog.

The fog was so thick, I couldn't even see my feet. I squinted into the murk in hopes to get a glimpse of what lie ahead. Suddenly, the mountainside flattened out into yet another ledge and I had just enough time to grab onto a rock pocket before the ledge ended. I heard the little rock ledge fall, then splash into the raging river below.

My breathing was shallow once again. "Okay. Well, look at the bright side: you didn't fall off of the edge, and you have avoided death twice now," I whispered.

I began to pull myself more onto the ledge. *BAM!* A crack had formed where the ledge touched the mountain. Panic rose inside me, then was replaced with a strange anger.

I looked up at the sky. "Before, it was scary! Now it's just plain ANNOYING! WHAT HAVE I DONE WRONG?" I screamed, "Eagle Spirit! You seem to always put me in deadly situations, BUT I SURVIVE! I know that you probably were expecting thanks, but NO! If you want thanks, STOP DOING THIS TO ME!!"

Crack! Crack crack! My yelling was causing the ledge to break off faster. I sighed in frustration; one more *crack* and I would fall into the river.

I might as well be walking through the doors of death.
AGAIN!

I rearranged my body so that when the final *'crack'* came, I would be prepared to jump off of the ledge into the river, and I waited for it to happen.

SNAP!

The rock ledge plunged through the fog and into the river. When I fell , I felt like the murk of the fog was trying to slow my fall. I turned my body to face the ground just as I hit the water.

Chapter 15

The water was ice-cold, but I barely had time to worry about that. As soon as I hit the water, the current pulled me under. I tried to swim back to the top, but when I was just about to reach it, I went down the rapids.

It was like falling down stairs, one after another. Just when I was about to recover from falling down a couple of stairs, I lost my balance and continued to fall. A couple more 'stairs' and I would reach the lower part of the treacherous river.

I rushed to the surface of the water and got in a few big breaths before I landed in the raging waterway. I don't exactly remember how, but as I was attempting to stay up on the surface of the water, I came across a piece of wood that I then used as a flotation device. Since the wood was keeping me afloat (barely though), I got a decent look at what lie ahead.

"Eagle Spirit have mercy," I gasped.

The river current sped up, but that wasn't what frightened me. Ahead, there were huge, bulging rocks jutting out of the water, and I was sure to hit one.

I tried to swim to the shore, but I hit the fast current sooner than I expected. The water rushed by me at first, then dragged me with it under the water. The bubbly river made it difficult for me see. I could see the pebbles on the riverbed, and the passing debris overhead, but nothing more.

Suddenly, a rock seemed to swim toward me like a giant black beast, and I tried to avoid it by swimming to the side.

But the current was strong. I hit the rock, expecting to break something, but my makeshift raft smashed against the rock instead of my body and shattered into splinters.

The good thing about this was that the wood shattered instead of my body. The bad thing was that nothing was keeping me afloat anymore. I felt like a rag doll being tossed around by the current. I had no control whatsoever as to where I was going or how my body moved; it was all in the hands of the current. I could, however, turn my body around to look up at the mountains.

> *Where are all of the demons? I would have thought Redskin would have warned the guards.*

I shrugged off the thought and turned my body around. Everything happened so fast after that. As soon as I turned, I hit a jagged black rock that was jutting out of the river. My kneecap slammed against it, and I knew that I had injured it. White hot pain shot through my leg like lightning: sharp, fast, and burning, filling my knee with the fire of a thousand suns.

Now I was desperate to get to shore. I *needed* to get to shore. I put every last drop of energy into getting to solid ground; paddling and flinging my arms in the water as if my life depended on it, which it did.

Finally, I felt the soft, wet sand in my hands. Weak with relief, I clawed my way up the riverbank and onto the damp grass of the woods. I was so happy to see the emerald grass, I grabbed a handful of it and rubbed the blades onto my face, not only because it was soft, but the smell—I love the smell of damp grass.

I pulled myself up into a sitting position, wincing as I did so. I looked down at my knee, which was covered in red blood.

"Deep breaths, Hazelnut. Deep breaths—OW!" I exclaimed as I attempted to extend my leg.

I need to clean it from infection, but how?

I glanced at the raging ice-cold river. *It's the only way.* Slowly, I scooted towards the water and settled myself in the soft, wet sand, lowering my bloodied leg into the river. The water felt like ice on my wounded knee, but I watched intently as it flowed around my injury, washing away the blood and dirt. I watched with disgust as a small pebble dislodged itself from my wound and was pulled a little ways by the current before sinking to the riverbed. I let out a sigh of relief.

I pulled my leg out of the soothing water and dragged myself to a nearby oak tree. I leaned against it, relieved to be in the pacifying serenity of the woods again.

I closed my eyes, heavy with exhaustion, and listened to the sounds of the forest: rabbits running around, birds singing songs to one another, woodpeckers *thump thumping* against the tree bark, the treacherous river raging past the shore. Something else stood out against the other noises, something that made my eyes shoot open and my back straighten up. The hairs on my arms rose in caution and out of instinct.

Voices. I didn't know whose voices they were, but they were familiar. They were drawing closer, and came from behind me. I heaved myself into the dense undergrowth and brush, staring with anticipation in every direction. I attempted to make out what the voices were saying. There were two of them.

"I'm absolutely certain I saw her out here."

"Really? Because we have been looking for almost an hour now and there is no sign of her."

"We must keep looking."

Shock and relief overwhelmed me as the voices' came into view. They were the last two people I expected to see, Desert Flower and Ocean Lotus. Weak with relief, I pulled myself out of the brush calling, "Desert Flower, Ocean Lotus! I'm over here!"

Both heads turned to look at me. For a moment, they looked confused, then wide smiles spread across their faces as they hurried to my side.

"Hazelnut! We thought the demons had killed you!" exclaimed Desert Flower. "I never thought that I would see you again!" Her voice cracked as she pulled me into a tight hug.

For a moment I closed my eyes, taking in the moment, then looked at Ocean Lotus, expecting to receive the same treatment. But she sat there looking bewildered, like she had no idea what I was doing in the forest. Twice she opened her mouth to say something, but quickly shut it. She kept looking at me, then Desert Flower. I myself was beginning to get confused as to why she was not jumping for joy.

I pulled myself away from Desert Flower's warm embrace, and looking at Ocean Lotus, asked, "Is everything okay, Ocean Lotus?"

She didn't seem to have heard me, but kept staring intently at me and Desert Flower.

"Ocean Lotus!" I exclaimed a little louder.

She heard me this time, and seemed to snap back to attention. "Who's Ocean Lotus?" she asked, looking bewildered.

"You, you numbskull!" shouted Desert Flower.

I was surprised at both of my friends' behavior. Ocean Lotus didn't know who she was and Desert Flower was shouting insults at her for it. I looked questioningly at Desert Flower. "What's going on? Why are you and Ocean Lotus acting so weird?"

Desert Flower was looking at me, but her eyes seemed unfocused and distracted. "I don't know what you're talking about."

Her eyes widened and her next words came out in a rasping breath, "How did you escape the demons?"

I began to shake my head and crawl away from the couple, but Desert Flower's arm shot out and grasped my bad leg beginning to pull me toward her.

"OW! Desert Flower, can you not see that you are hurting me? Let go!" I screamed.

Desert Flower's unfocused eyes bore into mine, and as she continued to pull, a menacing snarl broke out across her face. "Hazelnut, you should not have left the demons. Now Redskin will be out for your blood, and this time, you will not escape and you will watch Ashinders crumble because of your failure to save it. You will watch your family perish, along with the worthless mortals that we possess now. They will all be destroyed and then you will have nothing left. *Nothing.*"

My eyes widened in horror. I kicked at Desert Flower's hands with my good leg, striking her hands many times, but it did not seem to faze her.

After minutes of trying to free myself, I gave up. I had bloodied Desert Flower's hand without even trying. I did the only thing that I could think of.

"Help! Help! Somebody please help me!" I screamed at the top of my lungs. This seemed to shake Desert Flower and Ocean Lotus out of their terrifying haze.

"Quiet her, will you?" ordered Ocean Lotus with an irritated look on her face. It wasn't Ocean Lotus that spoke though, but a familiar voice that I had hoped to never hear again.

"Blueblood, get out of Desert Flower's body!"

Desert Flower snarled, "It took you long enough to figure it out."

"It was funny that you actually thought that we were your helpless puny *friends*. Then your tiny mortal brain finally figured it out," Ocean Lotus spat.

"Blackblood, it was *you* that gave away our cover!" Blueblood snapped.

"No it wasn't!" retorted Blackblood.

"*You* went into the haze, not me!" argued Blueblood.

"Do you think that I could have helped it? It's not my fault that Redskin possessed me!"

"Yes!"

"You are such a brainless demon! I couldn't help it!"

"Yes you could have!"

"No!"

"Yes!"

"No!"

While the two demons were arguing, Blueblood released my leg and I began to soundlessly crawl into the undergrowth. Once I had obscured myself from the demons, I listened to their futile argument.

"You are the reason that she figured it out," accused Blackblood.

"Um, no!" retorted Blueblood.

"You—" Blackblood stopped mid-sentence and looked around, realizing that I was gone. "—you let her escape!"

Both demons looked around frantically and stood up.

"Where did she go?" asked Blueblood.

Blackblood shrugged. "I don't know, but if we're going to find her we're going to have to shed these *costumes*. She already knows who we are, so why try hiding it anymore?"

Blueblood nodded in agreement.

Both demons started to glow and eventually I couldn't look at them because the bloodred light was too bright. Two bodies fell away from the glow: Desert Flower and Ocean Lotus. Both girls were limp and I wondered if they were dead. I desperately wanted to go see if they were okay, or drag them into the bushes and wait out the demons, but I knew that Blueblood and Blackblood would see and capture me if I attempted to do so. I could only watch.

The glow soon faded, and before me stood two demons. Blackblood's skinny body looked like a cornstalk compared to Blueblood's muscular figure. They both unfolded their massive black leathery wings and took to the skies. It took everything I had not to bolt out of the undergrowth to my friends' side and protect them from the monsters above.

Blueblood and Blackblood flew around the area for a couple of minutes. I pressed myself closer to the ground hoping that the brush would obscure me from the demons.

"Nothing!" Blueblood shouted to Blackblood.

"Me neither! I suggest we check the trail to the village, brother!" Blackblood responded.

Blueblood nodded and the two brothers flew north towards Ashinders.

Ashinders! Please don't hurt the villagers.

After the demons had flown out of sight, I scrambled to Desert Flower's side and pressed my ear to her chest. At first, I heard nothing, and grief overwhelmed me. Then, I heard a faint yet steady *thump thump, thump thump* and my grief was drowned with relief. "You're alive!" I rasped.

I stumbled over to Ocean Lotus' side and pressed my ear to her chest. Immediately, I heard her heartbeat, fast and consistent. They were both alive, even though their eyelids remained closed.

Weak with relief, I pulled Ocean Lotus over to Desert Flower and hugged them both. I wanted to lay next to them and relax, but I knew that we needed to get somewhere more sheltered. I looked behind me to where I had been hiding in the brush, then turned my head to the skies. No sign of the demons. I grabbed Desert Flower under the arms and heaved her into the undergrowth. After I made sure that she was well hidden, I crawled back to Ocean Lotus' side. As sweat began to trickle down my forehead, I laid back in the afternoon sun.

Suddenly, a bloodcurdling roar broke out in the distance, soon followed by screaming. *The demons!* I had almost forgotten about the monsters. I quickly seized Ocean Lotus under her shoulders and began to effortlessly drag her into the brush.

The lush undergrowth seemed feet away, but I soon felt the flowers of a gorse bush brush my foot. This gave me even more hope that I would make it, and I started to heave Ocean Lotus faster. Soon, all three of us were hidden in the thick green brush, me lying on my belly, and I peeked out into the clearing where we had been and suppressed a gasp.

Blackblood was standing in the middle of the clearing, a silver dagger in his hand. Blood dripped from its tip. The look on the demon's face was murderous, a bloodthirsty look in his eyes, his lips drawn back into a ferocious snarl.

Where is Blueblood? Did they fight? If so, I would have thought that Blueblood would have won; Blackblood was a living beanpole.

I watched intently and pulled Ocean Lotus and Desert Flower closer to me. I heard a rustle in the brush behind me and whipped my head around. Nothing was there.

Desert Flower stirred. Her eyes fluttered open. "What—" Before she could finish, my hand flew over her mouth.

"Hush!" I whispered in my quietest voice.

Another movement in the undergrowth behind me.

Probably just a frightened rabbit, I attempted to reassure myself, but my fear could not be subdued.

I warily turned my attention back to the clearing. Black-blood had disappeared. A fresh wave of fear and anxiety swept over me as I felt all my senses sharpen, but I heard nothing. All was silent.

Suddenly, something grasped me around my ankle and pulled into the thicker brush. Before I had a chance to look at who had grabbed me, I was swept into the air. I felt my head hit the rough bark of a tree trunk. My vision reeled and I felt like my stomach was being turned inside out by the gods.

As I was lifted out of the forest's canopy, Desert Flower's unfocused eyes met mine I saw my own fear reflected in her chocolate ones. She unsteadily reached out for me, even though I was feet above her, before collapsing from exhaustion as I lost all sight of the forest floor.

Chapter 16

I was hanging upside down as my kidnapper flew towards the ghostly Black Mountains. I knew whose face I would see even before I saw it. Blueblood. I should have known that he wasn't dead, but he looked uninjured, so who's blood was on the silver dagger that Blackblood had carried?

Please don't be the villagers

I saw Blackblood trailing behind me, a menacing sneer breaking across his face. I looked up to see that Blueblood was carrying me by my ankles, his expression blank. I thought I could detect a bit of regret in his eyes, but I'm sure I was just being silly.

I felt sick to my stomach as the winged demon lugged me toward the mountains. Everything was blurred, and blood poured from a wound on my forehead.

Suddenly my whole world seemed to flip upside down and my insides churned, then I vomited. The wind caught the vomit and blew it into Blackblood's face, causing him to stop flying in midair and go into a series of spitting spasms. I would have laughed but another wave of nausea swept over me and I hurled again. This time, Blackblood avoided the vomit narrowly and gave me a look of pure hatred.

I smiled at him, which angered him even more. Just as he began to swing his big fist at my face Blueblood flew upward and I felt the wind from Blackblood's fist brush the top of my head.

Blueblood spun around, fire burning in his eyes. "Redskin will have our heads if we bring her to him harmed," he shouted. "I don't want to die. I want to prove my loyalty to Redskin. Now I don't want you to lay another finger on the girl until we get back, and if you do, I will kill you myself." With that, he turned around and began flying toward the mountains again.

Blackblood quickly covered his sheer embarrassment with a snort of disgust and reluctantly followed Blueblood, all the fires of Hell burning in his eyes.

ONCE WE FINALLY reached the mountains, my stomach felt better, but my vision still reeled. I recognized the cave from which I had escaped before. Blueblood flew toward it. Before he could go into it though, Blackblood hurtled past him, landed smoothly, and ran out of sight.

"Moron," Blueblood growled. Once he too had touched down on the cave's smooth stone floor, he grabbed my wrist and put a familiar leather cuff around it. Only then did I notice that the previous one had come off—probably cracked when I collided with the rocks.

After he secured the cuff, he tossed me to the ground and sat down. He looked exhausted. For the first time, when his gaze locked with mine, crumpled and wounded on the cave floor, I saw pity in his eyes. And maybe even regret.

He turned away, looking instead at the tunnel Blackblood had dashed into. He sighed, turning his head back toward me.

"You know, the reason I do this—that we all do this— is to please Redskin, and to stay alive. If we don't follow his orders, he will kill us." He heaved another heavy sigh. "I just want to—" His voice trailed off as he remembered something. Something painful. Something lost. Suddenly, a thought came to my mind.

"Are there any female demons?" I asked.

Blueblood's eyes met mine, and there, in the red depths of his eyes, I saw pain, regret, and loss. "There were," he answered after an awkward moment of silence.

I knew I shouldn't have pressed on, but I couldn't help myself. "What does that mean, 'were'?"

"It's a long story, and Blackblood will be back with Redskin soon," he objected.

"Those are some pretty long tunnels," I remarked.

Blueblood sighed, "You're not going to give up, are you?"

"Not until I find out what you meant."

He shifted his position and took a deep breath. "I had a sister," he began. "In my eyes, she was the most beautiful demon in the whole world. Redskin met her, and I swear he thought that too. I loved her. He loved her. But he just *had* to keep his brutal reputation of killing. He made a rule that all female demons were to be executed at birth. But not her. I tried to, I tried—"

I wanted to hear more of the story, but I didn't want to push it because number one, he was a powerful demon; number two, I was his prisoner; and number three, I could tell it hurt him to even say this much, so it kind of made sense to leave it be. As you may have guessed though, from my previous experiences, I was more of a do now, think later type of person.

"Go on," I said, encouraging him tentatively.

"After she had her children, Redskin killed her. Poisoned her. She died in her sleep."

I could tell that he was on the verge of beginning to cry. I didn't want that to happen, not in front of a prisoner; that would be humiliating for him.

"I'm so sorry," I whispered. "That must have been—"

I was cut off when Blackblood came back into the room, Redskin just behind him. Blackblood snarled, "See! I told you he had gone soft! He was leaking information to the *prisoner*!"

"Quiet!" Redskin ordered.

Blackblood's snarl was immediately wiped off his face, and he cowered in the height and shadow of Redskin. Compared to Blueblood, he was a twig, but compared to Redskin, if you saw them from a different angle, you could mistake him for a cornstalk. I silently swore to myself that if indeed I ever truly escaped, I would tease him about that.

A small smile spread across my face.

"What are you smirking at?" Blueblood demanded, ignoring Redskin's growl of protest.

The smile dropped off my face as the demon approached me. Blackblood shoved past Blueblood, who tried to stop him. "Brother, if you do this, he will—"

"I have had it!" Blackblood growled as he raised a fist.

I scrambled backwards, remembering the steep drop off the edge of the cave. Redskin took a step forward. "Blackblood, if you touch her—"

His warning was cut off by my shriek of pain as Blackblood struck me across the face. He smirked. "That's what you—"

Blackblood's growl was cut off by his scream of agony as Redskin hurled him into a wall. The leader marched over to the stunned demon and grabbed the base of Blackblood's wings. The skinny demon yowled.

"I warned you," Redskin rumbled.

I watched in horror as Redskin pulled the wings off Blackblood. Blood splattered the stone walls and began pooling on the ground. The demon king dragged Blackblood to the opening of the cave, near where I was sitting, and tossed Blackblood off the edge.

The demon's shrieks echoed off the mountain as he fell.

Even though he was lost in the fog, I still heard the sickening *crunch* as Blackblood hit the ground.

I pulled myself away from the ledge, away from Redskin. Blueblood stared at the cave opening, his eyes brimming with tears, but as Redskin turned around, the muscular demon shook the sadness from his eyes and straightened up.

"What do you want me to do, sir?" Blueblood asked.

"Take the girl to Dr. Peterston," Redskin answered as he thundered back into the mountain.

"Sir, we've already tried, and it failed."

"And we'll try again. If it fails," he said turning, "we just kill her."

Redskin spun around and disappeared into the dim tunnel.

Blueblood heaved me to my feet—er, *foot*—and dragged me after Redskin. "He was my brother! You got him killed!" he growled.

My eyes widened. "*Me?*"

"You angered him!" Blueblood accused.

I thrashed in his firm grip. "Let me go! You know it's no use! You know that—" Blueblood placed a cloth in my mouth, muffling my words.

I kicked and struggled all the way to Dr. Peterston's office, which was a mess: papers scattered on the tables and desk; sketches and notes filled a board where the doctor stood analyzing his data. He jumped when Blueblood barged through the door.

Peterston stuttered, "B-Blueblood, so nice to see you again."

"Do shut up and get her ready for the test," Blueblood growled, tossing me on the floor at Dr. Peterston's feet.

The professor nodded and took my arm. "Where is Sir Redskin?"

"*King* Redskin to you," Blueblood corrected, "and he's on his way."

Peterston dragged me into the Possession Chamber, a room I had hoped to never see again. He attached the manacles to my wrists. Once he had me secured, he backed out of the room, slamming the door shut. *As if I can get out anyway* I thought bitterly.

A short time later, Dr. Peterston returned. Redskin was right behind him. "I'll leave you two alone," the short doctor muttered and exited the chamber again.

Redskin glared at me, the fiery depths of Hell reflected in his irises. "I was a little hopeful that when you fell off that cliff, you'd stay dead," he sighed, " but Eagle Spirit despises my ways; of course that birdbrain would let you live."

I narrowed my eyes. "I thought you wanted to use me for your—what do you call it—power capsule?"

Redskin rolled his eyes. "Of course I do, but at the time, you were *such* a nuisance. I was just fed up with you."

"Yeah sure, *I* was the annoying, unreasonable being in that scenario," I scoffed. Why did demons have to be so prideful?

"Don't accuse *me* of being unreasonable, child!"

"'Child?'" I repeated disbelievingly. "Um, I threw you halfway across this chamber *Mr.*"

Redskin drew his lips back in a snarl. "Quiet. Let us get this over with."

"It didn't work last time; why try it again?" I asked.

"It was just a coincidence that a magical force field appeared around you at the same time that I tried to put my magic inside of you," he said, folding his arms like it was obvious.

"Sure, sure," I muttered, trying to put on a brave face. But on the inside, I was terrified; what if this actually worked and Redskin was right about it being a coincidence, or will the force field come again? I didn't know how the magic had come to me, or if it was meant *for* me. If it came back, would I get hurt? Or even killed?

Redskin twisted the top off of a jar that he had been holding. I gasped. The glowing ball of orange and blue electricity hovered towards me, cold rolling off it in waves. Redskin raised his hand and the ball began to press against my sternum. I shivered as the sphere moved deeper into my body.

Redskin grinned menacingly. "Yes."

The sphere was completely submerged in my chest. Every bone and muscle in my body weakened. My head drooped. I stopped struggling from my chains as I heard Redskin's yowl of triumph.

"At last! I stand victorious!" he cackled.

Dr. Peterston peeked into the room. "Y-Yes sir, excellent sir. Um, can I go home?"

Redskin laughed, "I suppose I have no use for you anymore." He waved his hand and the doctor disappeared in a cloud of smoke.

Redskin flung the door to the chamber open wide and bellowed, "Demons! This is a cause for celebration!" I could feel the demons coming down the hall, echoing their leader's yowls of joy.

The next couple of hours went by slowly. Redskin had released me from my chains, but stationed guards at the entrance to the Possession Chamber. The demons brought out bottles of red and gold liquid, chugging it every once in awhile. I had never seen so many demons in my life; twenty filled the doctor's old lab, laughing evilly and throwing Dr. Peterston's lab research everywhere.

I sat in the dust, my wrists aching from the metal manacles. Redskin stomped into the chamber, followed by Blueblood. "I suppose you'd like some company," Redskin said in a mocking tone.

"I don't want yours," I retorted, "so go away."

Blueblood chuckled, "He doesn't mean *us*, child."

I raised my head and looked into Blueblood's eyes, which were the color of copper. "What?"

Redskin backed out of the chamber as the partying demons made way for two of their brethren, who were carrying something in between them.

My eyes widened. "B-Bloodriver?"

"Very good," Blueblood said as Bloodriver was tossed into the chamber. "Enjoy your little gift while he's still alive."

The door to the Possession Chamber slammed. I looked at Bloodriver, who laid at my feet. He looked up at me and I almost cried; I had never seen him this way, defeated, miserable. He had bruises and cuts all down his arms and legs. There was a moment of awkward silence.

"I-I thought y-you were—I didn't th-think I'd ever see you again," I managed, tears welling in my eyes. He pulled himself into a sitting position, his cow brown eyes looking directly into mine.

"Are you crying?" he asked, a smile breaking across his face.

"Maybe," I admitted as joyful tears rolled down my cheeks. As if through some sort of silent communication, we both embraced each other. I collapsed and sobbed into his torn shirt until it was soaked. He kissed my forehead, and I smiled up at him.

"Do you forgive me?" he asked. I sat up, grabbed the collar of his shirt, and pulled him in. An electric wave went through me as our lips met. I almost couldn't kiss him because I was smiling too much. "Of course I forgive you, idiot."

Bloodriver laughed softly and wrapped his arms around my waist. "Good."

Chapter 17

The door opened and Bloodriver and I separated. Redskin walked in. "Oh how cute!"

Bloodriver growled, his hand slipped protectively around mine, spreading his wings defensively.

Redskin rolled his eyes. "Please, Bloodriver. Stop pretending to be brave."

Bloodriver growled loudly, "Leave us alone."

"You've changed sides now, huh?"

"Father, please don't!"

Their conversation faded as a crazy idea came to me. I stood, ignoring Bloodriver's look of shock.

An image of Moonlight's body flashed across my vision, bringing tears to my eyes and filling my chest with anger and hatred.

"Redskin." I pushed away Bloodriver's wing. As I spoke, different images flashed in front of my eyes.

"You have destroyed families—"

Mother sobbing on the floor of our house, having just received the news of my death.

"—burned villages."

Ashinders going down in flames as the demons swooped overhead.

"You took my sister from me," I spat.

Suddenly, golden flames erupted in a circle around me, Bloodriver, and Redskin. Blue lightning arched from my torso, hitting Redskin square in the chest and sending him flying into the flames. He shrieked as holes burned through his wings. Before anything else could happen, Blueblood pulled his master from the flames.

During all of this, Bloodriver stared at me with a mixture of confusion and awe. I looked down at him, offering him my hand to help him up. Bloodriver took it and I pulled him up. We stepped out of the chamber. The party outside had ended.

Some demons stood holding bottles of the golden red liquid, confused. Some stood around Redskin, whose wings were still smoking. The rest growled at me and Bloodriver as we exited.

"So time to go," I whispered to Bloodriver, who nodded in agreement. He bared his teeth and we sprinted towards the exit.

Redskin's demons ran to stop us. Two of them launched themselves at Bloodriver. I flicked my wrist and they were sent sprawling into the mob advancing on us. Without warning, Bloodriver wrapped his arms around my waist. "Hold on to me," he said, a little too late. He spread his wings and flew at alarming speed down the hall.

I wrapped my arms around his neck and buried my face into his chest. We swerved and curved down halls and tunnels for so long I was afraid we had gotten lost. But then there was a light at the end of the tunnel and Bloodriver burst out of the mountainside.

I lifted my face and looked below us, my breath catching in my chest. Below us, the valley spread in a blanket of color. You could see the colorful tops of the market booths of Ashinders. To the west, the trees of the forest were turning beautiful shades of red, orange, and yellow due to the autumn. To the north, a river glistened in the bright afternoon sun, and to the east, a grassy meadow seemed to move in the wind; the variety of flowers bending in the breeze. An eagle soared about six feet to our left, its black eyes meeting mine for a split second before folding its wings into a dive, plummeting towards the treetops.

I smiled up at Bloodriver, and let out a squeal of joy as he dove after the eagle. Suddenly, Bloodriver let go of my waist, letting me fall through the air. I gasped, trying to turn to find him. "Bloodriver! It's not funny!" I yelled, but the words were whipped away in the wind.

Relief washed over me as I felt his hand around mine. I looked to my right and saw Bloodriver smiling at me. "Just enjoy it, Hazel; it's not everyday you get to fly."

I made a sharp retort that Mother wouldn't have approved of, but that too was lost in the air. Reluctantly, I spread my arms out.

"Do you mind if I help you out?" Bloodriver asked, mischief shining in his brown eyes.

I raised an eyebrow. "With what?"

"Living the full experience of flying, of course."

I wasn't sure what that meant. "Um, sure."

I felt a sharp prick in my back, quick like a needle. I swung my head around to look at my back and nearly screamed. I had two feathery eagle wings sprouting from my shoulder blades.

"What?" I looked at Bloodriver.

"Just relax. It's like having another set of limbs," he said.

Nodding, I closed my eyes, imagining my wings spreading, catching the wind. I abruptly stopped falling, the wind no longer stinging my eyes and searing my skin. My eyes opened and I found myself gliding over the trees, Bloodriver at my side. He still had my hand enclosed in his.

This. Is. Perfect.

Our wing tips brushed against each other as we soared over the trees. A clearing in the thick branches opened in front of us and we dipped our wings, gently gliding towards a grassy clearing.

Once we landed, my wings disappeared (which was kind of odd, but whatever). I walked to a nearby spring and quenched my thirst, relishing the cool water that ran down my throat. After I drank to my heart's content, I splashed water onto my face.

As I stared at my reflection, I noticed something off about my features. Realizing that my forest green irises were now a beautiful shade of gold, I splashed water into my face to make sure I wasn't dreaming.

I checked again. Nope; my eyes were the color of the afternoon sun.

"Bloodriver?"

He stood, shaking the water from his hair. "Yes?"

God, he's handsome, I thought.

"Uhm, er," Frustration snagged me as I lost my train of thought.

Bloodriver grinned, flexing his well defined muscles. "What? Are you distracted by something?"

I straightened by back. "I most certainly am not!"

He got down on one knee. "What are you so defensive about, then?"

"Well, I—I can't believe that you think I find your muscles attractive," I defended. "Your insanely good-looking, ripped muscles."

Bloodriver grinned his, 'I'm trouble but I'm going to cover it up with good looks' grin.

"Very well, whatever you say. Now, what were you going to ask me?"

I stood, flicking the water from my hands into Bloodriver's face. Pain flared in my ankle and I remembered it was broken. "Why didn't you tell me my eyes were gold?"

I limped over to a massive oak tree, studying the gaping hole between its roots.

"Two things: we were trying to fight off a tribe of demons,

and I didn't want you fretting over it. You actually look really attractive with golden eyes," Bloodriver replied.

As I turned to look at him, he shot to his feet. "I-I mean, the color really complements your—" He studied me. "Skin."

I raised my eyebrows. "You didn't tell me about my eyes because you think they complement my skin? And I thought boys couldn't get any stupider."

Bloodriver turned away. Was he blushing? *Definitely blushing.*

"There's a thick covering of moss in here. I think this should be enough room for the both of us for tonight," I said, gesturing to the space under the tree roots.

"You don't want to go back to Ashinders?" he asked.

I shook my head. "No, it would attract too much attention. I don't need to lose what family I have left."

"You have me," Bloodriver said, walking to stand by me. "Aren't I your family?"

I chuckled and butted my head against his arm. He turned towards me and I noticed blood bleeding through his shirt. "What happened?"

Bloodriver looked down at the wound. "I know I'm great and everything, but do you expect me to fight half a tribe of demons and come out unscathed?"

I rolled my eyes, turning my attention back to the tree roots. "Make yourself comfortable, I'm going to get us some food and healing herbs."

At this, Bloodriver grabbed my shoulder. "I'm not letting you go out by yourself," he protested. "Not after—" He winced in pain and clutched his left shoulder where the wound was.

I sighed, tearing the hem off my dress and wrapping it around his shoulder. "You, sir, are in no condition to travel. I will find the herbs *by myself.*"

Hesitantly, Bloodriver crawled under the roots, leaning

against the dirt wall. "I guess it *is* kind of comfortable," he admitted. I nodded, pushing aside a tree branch and disappearing into the forest.

Chapter 18

The herbs were easy to find. Marigold grew everywhere, and a great patch of borage sprouted right by the oak. I decided I would gather them later. It was the prey that was hard to catch, especially with a broken ankle.

I wish I had brought a hunting knife of some sort, and it probably would've been smart to make myself a splint.

An idea sparked in my head. Redskin's leather cuff that disabled my magic had been burned away by my golden fire wrath, so maybe I could summon a little something.

Closing my eyes, I put all my concentration into summoning a knife. When I opened them again, in my hand was a silver dagger like the one I had at home, but still no splint. Grinning, I crouched in the undergrowth, waiting for an unlucky rabbit or squirrel to strut by. Fortunately for me, a really fat rabbit heaved itself through the grass, its belly full from a recent meal. I threw my dagger like a spear, piercing the rabbit's spine. It fell to the ground. I retrieved my knife and the rabbit and began heading back.

A nearby juniper bush rustled, and I bared my knife, its blade catching the sunlight. From the bush emerged a stag, followed by a small fox.

My jaw dropped along with my knife and prey.

Father would come back as a stag, and Moonlight a fox.

"Father?" I looked at the stag, his black eyes comfortingly familiar. He nodded.

I got down(with difficulty) on one knee and looked at the fox. "Moonlight," I observed as the fox butted my leg affectionately. I stroked her soft fur. "How is this possible—I mean I know it's possible, but I never thought that the stories would come true."

The stag stepped forward and licked my forehead and touched his nose to mine. I smiled, tears welling in my eyes. "I miss you both."

The fox reared back on her hind legs, batting my chest softly. Her eyes were a beautiful shade of brown, just as they were when she was alive as Moonlight.

We're still here, dummy, giggled Moonlight's voice. It was soft and faint, like a summer breeze. I sighed and rubbed the fox's head, letting the orange fur run through my fingers.

The stag nudged the fox with his hoof, nodding towards the forest. Tail down, the fox turned and followed the stag into the woods.

I got to my feet, brushing the dirt off of my knee. After I gathered my knife and prey, I picked some marigold and borage and headed back towards camp.

When I arrived at the oak tree, Bloodriver was fast asleep slumped against the wall of the hollow. Grinning when I heard his snore, I silently crept to sit on his left and unwrapped his bandage. I was careful not to wake him. As soon as I unwrapped the bandage, I realized that in order to treat the wound properly, I would need to remove his shirt.

"Bloodriver?" I gently shook him.

He woke with a start, relaxing when he saw me. "What's up?"

I could feel my face grow hot with embarrassment. "Well,

in order to treat your wound properly, that would require the removal of your shirt."

Bloodriver smiled and nodded, pulling the shirt over his head to reveal the most muscular chest I've ever seen (abs included). It was all I could do to prevent my jaw from dropping. I straightened my back and began to chew up the herbs. I spat the pulp into my palm.

"This may hurt a little," I warned, rubbing the green paste in and over his wound. Bloodriver winced slightly, but he didn't seem to be in that much pain. Not like my ankle.

While I worked, I could feel his gaze on me. I had grown accustomed to fixing up wounds, as Father had often gotten injured in a silly way whilst he was out hunting. I tied the bandage around his shoulder again. "That should do it."

"Thanks," Bloodriver replied. "Now let's heal your ankle." He cupped his hands around my injury and a warm light erupted from between his fingers, warming my ankle and soothing the pain. When he removed his hands—those strong, amazing hands—my ankle felt brand new in the sense that the throbbing had subsided.

"Whoa." Awe spread across my face, making Bloodriver chuckle. "Thanks."

"No problem."

I held out the rabbit I had caught. "I got some food."

"Yeah, but I like mine cooked," Bloodriver complained playfully.

I narrowed my eyes. "Fine." Within the blink of an eye, the rabbit was cooked to perfection in my hand. "You eat your share first. I can wait."

Note to self: Bloodriver can *eat* when he's hungry. Once he was done, about seventy-five percent of the rabbit was gone, but that was okay; I wasn't that hungry.

After we ate, Bloodriver climbed out of the roots and turned, lending out his hand.

"What are we doing?" I asked, raising an eyebrow. I took his hand and he pulled me up. The sun had almost set, sending scarlet streaks spiraling through the sky.

Bloodriver wrapped his arm around my waist, taking my left hand in his. My hand slid up to his bare shoulder, careful not to touch his wound.

If he can heal a broken ankle, why can't he heal himself?

I pushed the question to the back of my head.

We moved away from the tree and began to dance. Not a fast, wild dance like the ones of Ashinders, but a slow, sleepy dance. A sway. "This, milady, is our first date," Bloodriver whispered.

"A date. While we are being hunted down by demons?" I questioned.

"It's perfect, isn't it?" Bloodriver laughed softly.

I lifted my head up and kissed him on the cheek. "Yes it is." That made him shut up.

He looked down at me, the fading sun turning his hair auburn. I touched my nose to his, a smile spreading across my face.

This time, Bloodriver wrapped his arms around my waist and drew me up to his lips. I almost couldn't kiss him because I was smiling too much. His great leather wings wrapped around me.

I pulled away and rested my head on his chest, a small yawn escaping from my mouth.

"Is someone sleepy?" Bloodriver teased. I nodded, not even flinching when he scooped me up in his arms and carried me to the tree. As he lowered me into the soft moss, I rolled out of his arms.

"What did you do that for?" Bloodriver asked.

"I can put myself to bed, thank you very much," I replied, glaring at him. Bloodriver sighed and laid down beside me. I shifted myself and put my head in the crook of his arm.

For a moment we both stared at the stars that were beginning to appear. Then Bloodriver turned his head and we kissed. Again. But this time, sparks flew; literally. Golden sparks were emitted from my body; tiny slivers of light swirling through the air, lighting up the tiny hollow like little fireflies. This was the most magical moment of my life, which was saying a lot considering what I'd been through.

Bloodriver pulled away, and the sparks faded. When I turned my head to the sky again, my breath caught in my throat. The stars gave off a blue glow, lighting up the sky like a great blue torch.

"It's beautiful," I said, breathless.

"I heard that the stars reflect their viewers," Bloodriver commented.

My eyes widened. "Where did you hear that?"

"Somewhere."

"Really? Where?"

"A friend." Bloodriver's eyes were copper in the starlight.

"Who is this friend?"

"Someone who was stupid enough to get his best friend kidnapped, and is trying to make it up to her."

I turned, looking at Bloodriver. "I think she forgives your 'friend'. But is she *just* a best friend?"

He sighed, tucking his arms behind his head. "He doesn't know; it depends if she thinks that they could be something more."

I propped my head up with my arm. "And if she says they could and should be more? What happens then?"

"Then he would agree, kiss her, and comment on how beautiful her eyes look when the starlight catches them, turning them silvery gold."

I laughed quietly as he kissed me. "Your eyes look beautiful when the starlight catches them, turning them silvery gold," Bloodriver murmured.

I laughed aloud this time, returning my head to rest in his chest. "I love you."

"I love you too," Bloodriver replied, taking my hand in his. I smiled, closing my eyes.

Before I knew it, morning was here. Sun shined through the roots, and the moss felt extremely comfortable under my body. I rolled over, surprised to see that Bloodriver wasn't there.

I can't believe last night actually happened; we kissed!!!

Blinking the sleep out of my eyes, I sat up, trying to peer through the roots to see Bloodriver, but I only saw the spring, and heard a muffled cry. I grabbed my knife and climbed out of the hollow, shock and fear gripping my heart. Bloodriver laid in the shallows of the spring, where the water was only a mouse length deep. His hands were bound behind his back, steely twine wrapped around his bat wings, tying them to his back. He stared at me, eyes round with terror.

My eyes widened. "Bloodriver? What the—"

"Hello Hazelnut."

I spun around, gasping when I saw the figure step out of the forest's shadows. "Redskin."

Chapter 19

My heart started pounding. "Get out of here. Those holes I burnt in your wings? There's a lot more where that came from," I warned.

Redskin smirked. "Fine, child. Challenge me all you want; your threats don't frighten me."

I remembered the chief's look or pure horror when he fell into the golden flames. The memory gave me confidence. "I could easily beat you in a duel."

Redskin raised an eyebrow. "Is that a challenge?"

"Well, not really, considering I'd beat you within the first ten minutes," I retorted.

"Sure you could," Redskin laughed, cracking his knuckles. "I suppose we'll need an audience." He waved his hand, and Bloodriver disappeared in a cloud of red smoke.

"No!" I turned to Redskin. "What did you do to him? Where is he?"

"Relax, child."

Bloodriver appeared a little ways away, sitting on a log, his face full of worry. I bet if he didn't have his gag in, he would've said some things to Redskin that earned him a mouthful of soap. Blueblood stood beside him, his expression full of hatred as his copper eyes burned into my skin.

Redskin snarled and sent a fireball speeding towards me. I turned away, closing my eyes, shielding my head with my hands, expecting a searing pain. As the fireball closed distance, a great shadow passed over me. The pain never came. I opened my eyes, surprised to see my eagle wings had returned and deflected the flaming orb. I moved them out of the way to see Redskin, his jaw hanging open. It would've been funny except for the loathing in his eyes.

"What?" he growled.

"I told you I could beat you," I said, launching myself into the air. I rolled into the federal position, forming a spherical shell around my body with my wings, so I must've looked like a huge feathered ball on the outside. Right before I hit the ground, I unfolded my wings, landing just behind Redskin. He spun around just in time to see my fist fly into his nose. The demon king doubled over, holding his royal nose. While he was in his short stage of pain, I kicked him in the groin.

It pleased me to see him collapse.

"Who says you can't win the *mortal* way?" I spat, readying my hand to hurl a fireball at him.

Suddenly, something hit me from behind. My fireball went out, my wings disappearing. Looking down, I saw sleek black tendrils coiling around my body. "Blueblood! This was a duel! That means two." A coil cut off my shriek.

Rage pulsed inside of me as Redskin recovered, glaring at me. I hated him, and Blueblood, and all other demons. I wanted them to stop messing with my life and my family. I wanted to be left alone.

Blueblood's coils started smoking and I realized that white-hot fire was curling off my body. Blueblood let out an agonized scream, his coils vanishing. I turned around, punching him in the face hard enough to knock him out. Stepping over his body, I rushed to Bloodriver's side, cutting at his bonds with my knife. As I was cutting at the metallic twine on his wings, I heard Redskin pounding towards me. I jumped, twisting in the air and extending my foot, catching Redskin in his right temple with my heel.

He crumpled, unconscious, to the ground. I went back to cutting at Bloodriver's ropes. Once his wings were free, he pulled away his gag, grabbed my hand, and we sprinted into the woods.

"That was a little excessive," Bloodriver commented.

"If I hadn't, you would still be tied up and I would be either seriously injured, getting beaten, or kicking Redskin's butt," I retorted.

"Good point."

My wings sprouted from my back again, and I took off into the skies, Bloodriver on my heels. He caught up to me in no time.

"Where to?" he asked, catching his breath.

"The Black Mountains," I replied.

"Didn't we just escape from there?"

"Correct."

"And now you want to go back?"

"Also correct."

"Willingly?"

"You are on a roll, Mr. Bloodriver." I smiled.

Bloodriver rolled his eyes. "You don't want to go back to Ashinders and tell your parents what you're about to do?"

"*Parent*. Singular noun. Father was killed. But to answer your question, no. Mother thinks I'm dead now. I don't want to go home, let her know that I'm not dead, then tell her that I might die. That would be redundant," I answered bluntly.

Bloodriver nodded. "What are we going to do there?"

"First, I want to wipe out a good portion of Redskin's army before King Pain in the Butt gets back. Then when he does, finish off what army he has left, then kill Blueblood, then His Majesty." My stomach twisted in knots.

"You planned this all out?"

"No, I thought it up while I kicked Redskin's face."

"Nice."

"Will you stand beside me?" I asked nervously.

Bloodriver took my hand. "Until the very end."

I smiled and turned my attention back to the Black Mountains, which neared us faster and faster. Letting Bloodriver take the lead, he landed in the cave in the cliffside (I'm just going to call it the cave) and waited for me to catch up before running into the twisting tunnels.

"We need to get to the room where the most demons will be," I called to Bloodriver, who nodded. We ran past several doors and caverns and finally came to a halt in front of a spruce door.

"Ready?" Bloodriver whispered.

I nodded, giving him a quick kiss before thrusting the door open. About fifteen demons stood on the other side, quietly conversing and drinking the red gold liquid (seriously, though? Is that some kind of demonic liquor?) A great glass window stood on the far side of the room, overlooking the valley. When me and Bloodriver opened the door, the room went quiet. Two demons dropped their glasses.

I unsheathed my dagger and charged the nearest demon, who shielded himself with his wings. I cut through the leathery material like wet clay. While the fiend howled in anguish, I kicked him through the window, not stopping to watch him plummet to his unfortunate death.

Half of the remaining demons charged me, the others advancing on Bloodriver. With my dagger in hand, I summoned a long golden sword in the other. I must look like a bad—you know, I'm not going to say it. I let the demons come to me. The nearest one was the first to get pierced by my sword, his limp body falling to the ground. I pointed to two demons, and golden twine laced itself between the two demons' wings, sewing them together.

Confused, the demons struggled to free themselves.

I grabbed the collar of one of them, and hurled the pair out of the window. Three down, twelve to go.

I looked at Bloodriver, who had an auburn spear in his hand, the tip ablaze. In the other hand, he held a rope, lashing it out at any demon dumb enough to approach him. Unfortunately, one was. The demon lunged at Bloodriver, who whipped the rope around the demon's wrist and catapulted the demon towards me. I moved out of the way, setting the flying demon's clothes and wings on fire as he sailed out of the window.

Eleven.

Two of the creatures advanced on me, and I cut through their torsos with my golden sword, shock spreading across their faces as they crumbled into dust.

Nine.

I panted, watching Bloodriver take on three demons at a time. His blade hit their necks one at a time. *Shinck, shinck, shinck.*

Six.

I felt a hand grab my shoulder, pulling me backwards. I was pushed into a corner, my knife clattering to the ground and my sword vanishing. I spun around. A demon lumbered towards me, a bold light in his eyes. He grabbed my arms at the elbows, holding them in place.

"What are you—" My question was cut short as he smacked his lips against mine, over and over again. He began to undo the lace in the back of my dress when I realized what he was doing. I kicked him in the crotch.

"You drunken idiot!" I screamed as I picked up my knife and stabbed his stomach, running towards Bloodriver.

Five.

Bloodriver fought valiantly, but his strength was waning; demons began piling on top of him, and clawing at him. Then one disintegrated into dust.

Four.

Something hurled into me from behind, knocking me over. My forehead slammed into the rock floor and red and purple spots danced across my vision, and I felt something sharp scrape and stab my back repeatedly.

I gasped, trying to pull myself away from this demon, but my strength was draining. My wings dropped to the floor and my eyes strained to stay open. I tried to bring my knife up to the attacker, but I felt a cold hand grab my wrist, twisting my arm around. I screamed.

Bloodriver looked over at me, his eyes widening. "Hazelnut hold—" He disappeared under a wreathing heap of furious demons.

"No," I managed. My head dropped to the ground. *To the very end.*

The cavern shook, but I didn't raise my head. Suddenly, the stabbing stopped, so did all of the shrieking and screaming. I heard the pounding of hooves, and the sharp yapping of a small animal. My vision blurred, but I felt someone turn me onto my back, and a purple red glow.

This is it; I am going to die. At least me and Bloodriver admitted our love.

"Bloodriver," I mumbled before my eyes rolled back into my head and I lost all consciousness.

Chapter 20

"Hazel! Hazel!"

My eyes shot open. Bloodriver sat with my head in his lap, concern filling his eyes. "Hazel! Are you okay?" His bare chest—that beautiful chest—was covered with cuts and scratches, and blood trickled around his eye from a cut above his eyebrow.

"Yeah. W-What happened?" I asked, sitting up. I blinked, unsure of what I was seeing.

"They came," Bloodriver and I said at the same time.

In the cavern, a herd of deer conversed silently with one another, ears twitching. Foxes wove in between them, barking quietly and grooming each other's wounds. One fox that was relatively small compared to the rest of the foxes hurried between her companions, squeaking worriedly. A fairly large fox padded towards the small fox, then barked at the small fox and dipped his head respectfully before padding to a lush furred vixen. The two touched noses with each other and then began licking each other's fur.

Meanwhile, in Deer World, a stag walked between his herd, sniffing for injuries. After he had checked everyone at least twice, he joined up with the small fox, and the pair approached Bloodriver and I.

Father, Moonlight," I greeted, nodding my head to each in turn. "Thank you so much for your help, but how did you get up here?"

We are spirits, child. We have certain powers, reminded Father's voice.

I smiled at the stag, who touched his nose to mine and looked at Bloodriver.

You remember Bloodriver, right? asked Moonlight.

Of course. I watched his progress while I was with Rose Petal, Father remembered.

Yeah! Isn't he great? I saw him and Hazel making out underneath the oak tree.

"Moonlight!" I scolded. "Can't a girl have some privacy without sisterly intercourse?"

Yeah, yeah, sure. Whatever. The fox leapt into my lap, poking her nose repeatedly into my stomach, making me giggle. "Stop that!" I pushed her nose away.

The fox licked my cheek and turned back to the stag, who turned to the herd of deer and foxes. With a bow of his head, the deer and fox disappeared in a flash of blue light. Then Father and Moonlight vanished as well.

I smiled, a tear rolling down my cheek. I sniffled, looking at Bloodriver. "Sorry, I don't usually cry like this."

I went to wipe away the tear, but Bloodriver took my hand, pushing the tear off my cheek with his thumb. "You're beautiful." He let his hand rest on my face.

I smiled, putting my hand over his. Bloodriver stood, helping me to my feet. He looked at the door. "Now we just need to find Redskin and Blueblood."

A bloodcurdling screech echoed down the hall. "I WILL END YOU!"

I muttered, "I think we did." We sprinted out the door, dashing down the hall. We turned a corner and I saw Redskin and Blueblood hurtling towards us. "I've got Blueblood," I said. "Whatever happens, just know I love you."

Bloodriver nodded. I smiled, turning my attention back to the demons. I leaped over Blueblood's head, nicking his back with my knife. That made him angry. He spun around, a growl rumbling in his throat. "I swear—"

He didn't have time to finish his threat; I smacked him in the chest with my foot. "It's not nice to make threats!" I taunted as I sprinted down the hall.

I heard Blueblood snarl and pound after me. I ran faster, halting when the tunnel opened into the cave. Spinning around, I bared my knife, the golden sword appearing in my hand. Aur the Golden Sword.

Blueblood stopped, panting, a wild light dancing in his copper eyes. "I should've killed you a long time ago."

Aur the Sword glowed menacingly. "Now's your chance," I said, getting rid of Aur and sheathing my knife. "Kill me."

Blueblood snarled, "Foolish girl!" and launched himself at me. I stepped to the side, watching with pleasure as Blueblood face-planted into the rock floor.

"I thought demons were accurate with everything," I teased.

Blueblood stood, dusting off his pants. He ran up to me and swung at my face, which I dodged. When I stood again, Blueblood had two long knives in his hand. He screamed a battle cry and herded me towards the lip of the cave. I turned, panting, and sprinted towards the edge. Then I did the most stupid thing ever.

I jumped.

I fell through the air, panic fighting to control me, but I wouldn't let it. I closed my eyes, trying to block out the oncoming rushing river. I put all my focus into my inner powers and felt the air stop slicing into my face, whipping my hair into my eyes. When I opened my eyes again, my eagle wings had caught the air and I ascended.

When I was high enough to peer into the cave, Blueblood was making his way back to the tunnels, twirling his knives like batons. He threw one high above him, but he missed me and it clattered across the floor, skidding off the edge. I dove for it, hearing Blueblood's gasp as he realized he was missing a knife.

In air, I caught hold of the hilt, flying back towards the cave. Blueblood had leapt into the air, flying circles above my head.

"If it's an aerial battle you want, it's an aerial battle you will get," I muttered to myself. I threw his knife high into the air, satisfaction seizing my heart as I heard a pained, angry scream. Blueblood dove towards me, hands outstretched.

"For Ashinders!" I cried as I flew to meet him. He drew his other knife and swung it at me. I balled my fists and whirled them towards the blade.

Just before flesh met metal, Aur appeared in my hands, and our weapons clashed—blade on blade—with the loudest sound I'd heard in a long time. I drew my sword back for a second strike, and with all my might, thrust my sword at Blueblood.

His wing folded in front of his face, but Aur went through them with no problem. Blueblood howled and began to fall through the sky. After he got over the shock, he unfolded his wings, and (to my amazement) began unsteadily gliding towards the ground. He turned and smirked at me.

"You thought you could defeat me that easily?" he goaded. "What an—"

He was cut off as a great gust of wind blew him into the mountainside, a sharp spire of rock stabbing him right through the torso. Blood welled in the wound, and as Blueblood stared down in shock at the rock jutting from his stomach, a rumble shook the mountain, sending a massive boulder tumbling towards Blueblood, who was speared to the mountainside. The rock smashed into the demon, sending it, one screaming demon, and the spire tumbling into the bubbling rapids below. My jaw dropped when I saw the small glitter of his knife, which got washed up on the shore. A transparent figure appeared next to it, picked up the blade, and smiled up at me. It was Rose Petal, her long lush hair flowing over her shoulders. I dipped my head to the goddess. She tucked Blueblood's knife into the folds of her robes and vanished with a silver light.

I flew back up to the cave and was completely shocked to see Bloodriver and Redskin fighting in the small cavern, sending balls of magic flying at each other. I started towards Redskin, but something compelled me to spectate for now. I flew into the cave, sitting against the wall.

Both beings were bruised and bloody. Redskin had a great cut along his chest, and Bloodriver had opened his shoulder wound again, the scent of marigold and gore filling the cave.

Redskin fought with the fires of the underworld, literally. He had flames surrounding his body, coming out his nose, and filling his irises. On the other hand, Bloodriver was losing stamina. His aim was terrible, and he barely had time to get out of the way before Redskin torched him. I wanted to jump in so bad, and it wasn't helping that Aur gave off his self-confident shine again. "Stop that!" I quietly scolded the sword, which made me feel stupid, but the glow stopped, replaced by an agitated shudder. Resting the blade against the wall, I looked back at the fight and nearly lost my marbles.

Bloodriver was being backed into a corner, receiving blow after blow from Redskin, who was having no mercy. With each strike, Bloodriver convulsed and let out an agonized scream.

I couldn't take it anymore.

Grabbing Aur, I advanced towards Redskin. A glowing figure appeared, blocking my path. Her dark hair gleamed in the sunlight, her eyes glowing.

"You cannot help him, child," Rose Petal said. "It is his battle, not yours."

I glared at her. "But he's losing! He'll be killed!"

"It's his battle."

"You already said that!"

Rose Petal narrowed her eyes at me, her voice resonating around the room, "Do not protest against a god, Hazelnut. It is not wise. I will say this one more time: this is not your battle, it's Bloodriver's."

Neither Redskin nor Bloodriver seemed to notice the goddess's presence. I dropped my head, going to sit by the rock wall again. "It's just—if he died, I would never forgive myself. Especially if there was something I could do to prevent it," I whispered shakily.

Rose Petal sat down beside me, wrapping her arm around my shoulder. "I know," she sighed. "I'm not supposed to tell you this, but he won't die today."

I looked at her, wiping tears from my cheeks. "You know that for sure?"

She gave me that look, *I'm a goddess and you're questioning my knowledge?*

I smiled sheepishly, looking back at the battle. Redskin had a knife drawn, raising it to deal the final strike to Bloodriver. All of my heart said to run towards Redskin with Aur in my hand, stab him to death, then kiss Bloodriver and return home to Mother, Desert Flower, and Ocean Lotus. Maybe I could have Ocean Lotus make me a nice bowl of oatmeal, and some fresh orange juice. The thought made my stomach growl.

Bloodriver sat on his knees, his hair in his face and sweat pulsing from his forehead. Redskin cackled, "You were a fool to think you could beat me, and the girl. Well, she is a pure weakling.

I scowled at this remark.

Bloodriver panted and glared at Redskin, an unnatural fire burning in his irises, and the cavern's temperature went up about ten degrees.

Suddenly, a copper light erupted next to Bloodriver, taking on the form of a six foot falcon. The bird's eyes stared straight at Redskin, its sharp beak glistening menacingly.

"*Dinistrio,*" Bloodriver hissed. *Destroy.*

The falcon cawed and took off, flying straight through Redskin and out of the cave.

Redskin's look of pure shock quickly changed to a smirk. "Looks like your little magic trick didn't work after all." He put on a fake pouty face.

"Duck," Bloodriver said.

"Excuse me?"

Bloodriver pointed to something behind his father.

The massive falcon was flying towards the cave with incredible speed, its talons outstretched. Bloodriver ran straight for me while Redskin stared at the bird. He grabbed my wrist and pulled me to the ground so we were both flat on our bellies. "Watch this."

The falcon slammed Redskin into the wall, and since the bird was a spirit you could say, it went into the wall without leaving a mark. Redskin slid to the floor, blood dripping from his back.

I thought everything was over, but Bloodriver's expression told me otherwise. "*Bwyta,*" he murmured. "*Consume.*"

The falcon came bursting out of the wall again, grabbing Redskin around the shoulders and swooping out of the cave. I stood and ran to the cave's edge, watching the ghostly bird.

Redskin was tossed into the air like a doll, and the falcon snatched him up in its great beak. The most disturbing thing was that you could see Redskin inside the bird so it seemed like His Majesty floated in the air.

The bird let out a massive caw as Bloodriver joined me at

my side and took my hand. "Thank you," he said, dipping his head.

Its aura glowing brighter by the second, the bird screeched and Redskin screamed as his demonic body disintegrated like a sand castle in a storm.

Bloodriver covered my eyes right as the falcon exploded in a copper light, lighting up the entire valley (which is to say, *a lot* of land). When I uncovered my eyes, the world literally seemed to get brighter, more colorful. Puffy clouds danced across the sky and fluffy snow began to fall from the sky. We flew down into the forest.

"Isn't a happy ending supposed to result in sunshine and everyone happy and smiling?" I frowned up at the sky.

Bloodriver wrapped his arms around my waist. "It *was* sunny, and right now, I'm the happiest person in the world." He started blushing. "And I would be even happier if you would be my wife."

I stared at him for a moment, astonished. Then I wrapped my arms around his neck and drew his lips to mine. "Of course I will." Tears of joy rolled down my cheeks.

We stood there, kissing, snow dusting our hair, but at the moment I couldn't care less; I had just survived an extremely perilous adventure with my best friend who just proposed to me.

I couldn't care less.

Epilogue

Twelve years later exactly, me and Bloodriver walked down the cobblestone path connecting the market to the village. The townspeople had grown used to Bloodriver being a demon—well, half demon—so everything was at peace.

Snow dusted the rooftops and warm light poured out of almost every window. As we neared our brand-new four bedroom house, I heard excited squeals sound from inside, and two children—a boy and girl—tumbled out of the door sending snow into the air, rushing towards us, followed by Desert Flower, who held a baby boy in her arms.

"How was the market?" the little boy asked, his forest green eyes gleaming.

"Yes, did you get us anything?" prompted the girl.

Bloodriver got down on one knee, opening a leather satchel. "Why, indeed I did," he remarked, poking them in the stomachs.

The children giggled excitedly. "I want mine first!" the boy demanded.

"Now, now, Oak River," I chided, "be nice to your sister; but I suppose we can save the best for last."

Oak River looked hurt, but he pushed his black hair out of the way and cupped his hands. "I'm ready to receive my gift!"

Bloodriver drew a small wooden sword from the satchel and gave it to Oak River, who bounced up and down happily.

"Thank you Father! Thank you! Could you maybe give me lessons later?" he asked hopefully.

Bloodriver leaned into Oak River. "Yes, and between you and me, I think I have more skill than your Mother ever will," he stage whispered, looking straight at me.

"Excuse me! Who helped you defeat the demons?" I asked.

"I don't remember."

His reply was cut short as four more kids ran out of our house, barreling into him and I.

"Tell us the story again!"

"Pleeeeease?"

"Yes, please?"

Ocean Lotus emerged from the house, shooing the kids away. "Dakota! Astraya! Get off your aunt and uncle!"

Two curly-haired girls stepped away, heads down. "Sorry, Mother."

Desert Flower came over to the commotion, managing to help me to my feet despite having a child in her arms. "Sorry about that," she said. "My children are usually more well-behaved than that." She gave a dark haired boy and a sandy blonde girl a stern look. "I was just about to put Sonny down for a nap." She looked at the boy in her arms.

I smiled at Sonny (who's nickname is short for Sun Stream), who sucked his thumb sleepily. "You go do that, and we will entertain the kids for you."

"Oh thank you," Desert Flower said, hurrying off to her house further down the road.

"All kids inside!" I chuckled as the kids began to mock fight with Bloodriver. At once, they obeyed, but my daughter, Moon Song, stormed up to me. "What about me? Father didn't give me *my* gift! Just because Oak River just turned six doesn't mean—"

"Calm down, Moon Song," I soothed. "Your Father was just saving the best for last." I raised my voice, "Weren't you, Bloodriver?"

At his name, Bloodriver sat up. "Yes? Oh, yes." He grabbed his satchel and pulled out a silvery blue pendant wrapped in gold. It looked like golden ivy was growing around it.

Moon Song ran over to the pendant, her silver eyes glowing as Bloodriver put the necklace on her, letting it rest on her chest. "See? It's beautiful. Just. Like. You." With the last three words, he poked her stomach, making her let out a high-pitched laugh. Moon Song ran inside, followed by Astraya and Dakota, who both admired her pretty necklace. Oak River began go inside, but turned, signaling to the two children who wrestled with Bloodriver.

"Flame Fall! Violet! Come on!" he called. The kids raced into the house.

I chuckled, helping Bloodriver to his feet and picking up his satchel. "Come on, it's storytime."

When we got inside, I found the kids sitting on our living room rug, grouped around the couch. I sat down, Bloodriver making himself comfortable in a nearby chair. Moon Song climbed into his lap, lying down with her head resting on his belly, turning the pendant around and around in her hands. Bloodriver gestured for me to begin.

I inhaled and exhaled calmly, waiting for Astraya to climb onto the couch, laying her head in my lap.

"Where should I start?" I asked the audience.

"The very beginning!" Moon Song requested ardently.

"Yes, before the attack!" agreed Violet, casting a sideways glance at Moon Song, who absentmindedly braided her chocolate hair.

I smiled. "The *very* beginning?" I asked, laughing when all of the kids shook their heads vigorously. "Alright, alright. A rustle in a nearby bush caught my eye, I drew back my bowstring and waited."

SIGMA'S
BOOKSHELF

Sigma's Bookshelf (www.SigmasBookshelf.com) is an independent book publishing company that exclusively publishes the work of teenage authors, who are between the ages of 13 - 19. The company was founded in 2016 by Minnesota teenager Justin M. Anderson, whose first book, *Saving Stripes: A Kitty's Story*, was published when he was 14, and has since sold hundreds of copies.

"I know there are a lot of other teenagers out there who are good writers and deserve to have their work published, but don't have access to the kinds of resources I do. I wanted to help them," he said.

Sigma's Bookshelf is a sponsored project of Springboard for the Arts, a nonprofit arts service organization. Contributions on behalf of Sigma's Bookshelf may be made payable to Springboard for the Arts and are tax deductible to the extent permitted by law. Donations can be made online at www.SigmasBookshelf.com/donate.